"Are you pregnant?"

Duncan's voice boomed from the doorway where he stood holding up a pink-and-blue box. "Is that what this is for?"

A flush inched up Samantha's throat to her face. "It's a home pregnancy test—but it's none of your business!"

His eyes raked her body. "You fainted.... Your breasts are larger, and your belly—" He noticed her hands instinctively cup her belly and she lowered her head. "Get on with it. Take the test."

When Sam had followed the instructions carefully and sat down at the table, Duncan sat opposite her. Neither said a word until the timer went off.

"I'll go look," she muttered.

She peeked down at the receptacle...and stared at the big and very blue dot. "Oh, God..." She leaned against the wall as the room seemed to spin around her. "What am I going to do?"

"I know what you're going to do," said Duncan. "You're going to marry me."

ABOUT THE AUTHOR

With over eight million copies of her books in print
worldwide, Barbara Bretton enjoys a warm place in the
hearts of romance readers everywhere. After thirty-plus
contemporary and historical novels, this bestselling author
is listed in *Foremost Women in the Twentieth Century*, and
has been honored with numerous writing awards, including
Romantic Times Reviewer's Choice awards and a Silver
Pen Award from *Affaire de Coeur*. Barbara is a two-time
nominee for the *Romantic Times* Storyteller of the Year.
She loves to hear from her readers, who can reach her at:
P.O. Box 482, Belle Mead, NJ 08502.

Books by Barbara Bretton

Barbara Bretton

OPERATION: BABY

Harlequin Books

TORONTO • NEW YORK • LONDON
AMSTERDAM • PARIS • SYDNEY • HAMBURG
STOCKHOLM • ATHENS • TOKYO • MILAN
MADRID • WARSAW • BUDAPEST • AUCKLAND

For Deby, with love and gratitude

"It's ill wark, takin' the breeks aff a Hielandman."
—Unknown

ISBN 0-373-16689-3

OPERATION: BABY

Copyright © 1997 by Barbara Bretton.

This edition published by arrangement with Harlequin Books S.A.

Printed in U.S.A.

Chapter One

Scotland

He was tall.

He was dark.

And he was naked.

Right there, in the passenger cabin of the plane.

"Speak up, lassie," the naked man said. "I don't understand a word you're sayin'."

No surprise there. Samantha Wilde, thirty-two years old and Harvard-educated, was struck dumb with shock. The last thing she'd expected when she boarded the small plane was to find the pilot naked as the day he was born. She tried to say something but no sound came out. What on earth did you say to a naked Scotsman, anyway?

"You're wasting my time, lassie," the man said. "If it's looking you're after, then look your fill and say goodbye."

Sam tried to say something. She really did. But there was something about being faced with so much male splendor in a confined space that rendered her speechless. It wasn't that she'd never seen a naked man before, even if it had been a long time between sightings. She was as sophisticated as any other American woman at the end of the twentieth century.

The male form in all its infinite variety didn't usually make her feel like swooning, but this time she found herself grabbing on to the sides of the cabin door for support.

She thanked God her view was partially blocked by one of the two seats in the tiny passenger cabin. If he stepped into the aisle, she'd probably have a heart attack. Back in Houston, the hometown papers would have a field day with the headline. Jewelry Executive Dies at Feet of Naked Man.

Things like this simply didn't happen in her orderly, well-organized life.

"I—I, um—" she stammered, reduced to the communications skill level of a three-year-old. "Th-they told me I could find a pilot here who would b-be willing to take me north."

His dark brows shot together in a fierce scowl. "They told you that, did they now?"

"Well, yes," she said, wondering when he was going to remember he was naked. "I asked at the office and they told me I'd find you out here."

"Aye," he said, nodding slowly. "A logical assumption."

"I'll pay you twice your normal rate," she volunteered, making sure she maintained eye contact. It would be too easy to stare at him as if he was her private centerfold come to life. "I have to reach Loch Glenraven by nightfall."

"Loch Glenraven?" He looked at her with obvious

curiosity. "And what would be taking you to such a place?"

"Business." Not that it was any of his. He should be more concerned with catching a cold, what with all that exposed skin.

"One hundred twenty people live in Glenraven, and most of them raise sheep." His dark blue eyes studied her from sole to crown. "You haven't the look of a shepherd about you."

"Do you want the job or don't you?" she asked, trying to pretend she negotiated with naked Adonises every day of the week. "I'm sure one of the other pilots would be glad to fly me up to Glenraven."

"There are no other pilots, lass. I'm the only one here today."

"Fine," she said. "Then name your price."

His laugh was an alarmingly erotic rumble. She couldn't remember the last time she'd been so aware of a man, clothed or otherwise. "My price is more than you could handle."

"Try me," she said, then instantly regretted the challenge when she saw the look in his eyes veer from amusement to speculation. *Try me.* What kind of insane thing was that to say? She must have lost her mind. "What I mean is—"

"Ten thousand American dollars."

"You're joking."

"Those who know me know I never joke about money. Ten thousand American dollars."

"That's highway robbery."

"Call it what you will, lass, but that is the price."

Naked and crazy. There was a winning combination for you. "I'd rather walk to Glenraven."

"Then you'd best get started," he advised, "for it still grows dark early this time of year."

"Your advice would carry a lot more weight if you had your pants on," she snapped, turning toward the door. "Thanks for your time, but I'll find Glenraven by myself."

FROM THE MOMENT Duncan Fraser Stewart opened his eyes that morning, he'd had the sense all was not right in his world. First there was the row with Old Mag, his housekeeper, about the amount of haddock one man could eat at a sitting. She served up meals by the pound, not the plate. He had no doubt they could feed all of Glenraven on a week's leftovers.

"I cook for families," Old Mag had said fiercely. "Not for one lone man." Her unsubtle way of reminding him that he was thirty-seven years old and without wife or offspring.

"Do what you want, old woman," he'd roared. "I'll take my meals at the pub until you come to your senses."

Lucy at the Heather and the Thistle knew better than to question him before he'd had his mug of strong tea. After breakfast, he'd flown his plane to Glasgow to speak with his European agent and had been on his way back to Loch Glenraven when a nasty oil leak forced him to land at this little highland outpost.

They were woefully ill-equipped, so he'd done his best with what he had on board, a messy and unpleasant job to say the least. Still, he'd managed to cobble together a temporary solution, one that would at least get him home in one piece. A storm was brewing to the west and his window of opportunity would not last long.

He kept a change of clothes stashed in a duffel behind the pilot's seat and had been changing into them when the American woman surprised him.

He knew her nationality before she opened her mouth and he heard that soft drawl. She had that lean, rangy look he associated with Americans. A result, no doubt, of all that corn-fed beef and huge mutant vegetables they fed their children over there. Long lustrous blond hair. Big clear blue eyes framed by dark lashes and brows. Not a scrap of makeup that he could see. She had the kind of beauty that would age like the finest whiskey.

It was hard to imagine what might bring a woman like that to Glenraven, but he was going to find out.

SAM DREW IN a calming breath and tried again. "I need to get to Loch Glenraven," she said slowly and carefully into the phone as a chill wind whipped her hair across her cheeks. "Can you help me find a car and driver?"

The woman on the other end of the line said something, then paused, obviously waiting for Sam to respond. Sam wanted very much to respond but she hadn't understood more than every third word. She wondered if the Scotspeople she'd met were having as much trouble understanding her as she was having understanding them. Sometimes she had to remind herself they were all speaking the same language.

"Please," she begged. "Jock drove me here. Could he possibly—"

The word no came through loud and clear.

"Damn," she whispered, pressing the off button on her cell phone. Now what was she going to do? The airfield's office was locked. The clerk had apparently closed up for the day while Sam was talking to the naked pilot. And why shouldn't he close up? She'd seen Texas ghost towns that were more active than this little airfield. With a storm kicking up, they probably wouldn't see another soul all day.

She turned toward the crumbling runway. The naked pirate and his Cessna were still there. The thought of paying ten thousand dollars to go the hundred miles or so to Glenraven galled Sam no end, but she didn't seem to have a choice. It was either pay that outrageous sum or spend the night alone in the middle of nowhere with nothing but her cell phone and her imagination for company.

And, to make matters worse, dark threatening clouds had settled over the mountains.

Besides, she hadn't come this far to give up now. With a little luck, by this time tomorrow she'd have her elusive prey's signature on the bottom line of an exclusive Wilde & Daughters Ltd. contract. That was worth whatever embarrassment she'd feel when she told the naked Scotsman she'd pay his ten-thousand-dollar ransom to get to Loch Glenraven.

She marched to the plane and was about to hoist herself into the cabin when he appeared in the doorway. He was fully dressed except for shoes and socks. Wouldn't you know it? Even his feet were gorgeous.

"It's a deal," she said without preamble. "Ten thousand dollars to fly me up to Glenraven right now."

If her decision surprised him, he didn't let on. The

expression on his darkly handsome face didn't change.

"You'll pay me ten thousand dollars to take you to Glenraven."

"It's highway robbery, but yes, I will."

"And what is there in Glenraven that interests you so much that you'll surrender to highway robbery to get there?"

"That's none of your business," she said evenly. "Will you take me there or not?"

He hesitated. "There's little in the way of amenities at Loch Glenraven," he said. "It's a small town and a tightly knit one. Strangers are looked upon with suspicion."

"That won't be a problem," she said with just the right note of hauteur in her voice. "I'm expected." Which, of course, she wasn't.

"I know everyone at the Loch and all their friends and relations," the pilot said. "Which one of them expects you, lass?"

His obvious distrust was getting on her nerves. "Bad enough you're getting ten thousand dollars of my money," she snapped at him. "You don't deserve my itinerary, too."

"Angus Birkell?" he asked.

She shook her head.

"Robbie Macdonald?"

"No," she said, as her tenuous hold on her temper began to slip.

"It couldn't be Simon Laidlaw. He's on his honeymoon with the Widow Leslie. Conn Thripp is in hospital. And old Tom wouldn't be the kind of man you'd—"

"Duncan Stewart," she burst out, unable to bear his patronizing scrutiny another second. "If you must know, I'm going to see Duncan Stewart."

THE LASS'S NAME was Samantha and she claimed she had a six o'clock dinner appointment with Duncan Stewart at the castle.

Which was news to Duncan Stewart.

"Why are you staring at me like that?" she demanded. "Is it so hard to imagine I might have an appointment with Mr. Stewart?"

Duncan nodded his head slowly. "Aye," he said. "Harder than you might think."

She seemed to gather strength from his momentary surprise. "So will you fly me up to Glenraven?"

"I'll fly you to Glenraven," he agreed. What better way to discover why the beautiful American businesswoman was on her way to breach the walls of his castle?

She extended her right hand. "Ten thousand dollars, American."

He clasped her hand in his. Her fingers were long and graceful, her bones delicate. He could crush them with little pressure. "Ten thousand dollars, American."

She allowed herself a quick smile. "It's a deal."

He allowed himself to notice what a beautiful smile it was. For a long time now he had gone out of his way to ignore such things. "We'd best get on with it," he said, still holding her hand in his. "There's a storm on its way."

She glanced at the sky, and her clear blue eyes

widened in alarm as she saw how quickly the dark clouds were approaching. "It's not that I'm afraid to fly," she said, squaring her shoulders. "I just don't believe in taking unnecessary chances."

He hardened his heart against her display of courage. "'Tis my fondest wish to die in bed of old age. I'll not be meeting my Maker in this bucket of bolts."

She relaxed a little. "I'm glad to hear that."

"Then give me your other hand, lass, and let's be on our way."

She extended her left hand and he took that one, as well. With one easy motion he swept her up and into the cabin.

"Oh!" She stumbled against him, her breasts brushing lightly against his chest. Spots of color appeared high on her cheeks and she ducked her head.

It surprised him to note that he still held her hands firmly in his. He released her and took a step backward. "Sit next to me," he advised. "The ride will be smoother up front."

"No, thank you." Her tone was firm. "The passenger seat is fine with me."

"We'll be flying into some choppy air. The ride is smoother up front."

"Back here is fine with me."

"You'll be changing your mind soon enough."

"I doubt that." He could hear the edge in her voice. The businesswoman had once again banished the more vulnerable woman.

"It's an hour flight," he said, striding toward the cockpit. "We'll see where you end up."

SAM HAD LIKED HIM better when he was naked and mute.

She'd grown up with a father who believed he knew what was best for his three daughters, everything from what kind of toothpaste they used to whom they would marry and when. Lucky Wilde had even issued an ultimatum, demanding that his girls marry by year's end or lose their inheritance. Her sisters might get themselves all worked up over their father's edict, but Sam would never pay attention to nonsense like that. As far as she was concerned, marriage and slavery were synonymous and she wanted no part of either one.

She'd watched her father move from marriage to marriage, testing wives the way Goldilocks tested porridge. Her mother had been his first wife—and the only one to walk out on him.

He'd been a faithful husband to Julia. Truth was, he'd been faithful to all of his wives. Julia, however, hadn't felt obliged to return the favor. She left Lucky Wilde six months before their second anniversary, leaving behind their year-old baby girl. Julia remained a strong presence in Sam's life, but Sam grew up under Lucky's watchful eye.

There had been some rocky times during her adolescence when her need for freedom clashed with his need for control, but somehow she had managed to stand up to her powerful father and enter adulthood with her independence intact. After that, standing up to this arrogant Scotsman should be a piece of cake.

She strapped herself into one of the two narrow passenger seats while he prepared for takeoff. The engine clattered to life and she tried to ignore the tinny sound as the propellers whirred madly outside her window. Rain pinged against the glass, blown horizontal by a gust of wind. It must have started while she was fastening her seat belt.

She leaned forward in her seat. "Excuse me," she called out over the clanking engine. "Are you sure you should be taking off in this weather?"

He turned in his seat and fixed her with a dark-eyed look. "What weather?"

"What weather?" Her voice rose in surprise. "There's practically a gale blowing out there."

"A fine April day in Scotland," he said. "The real storm is still miles away."

"My father's pilot would never take off in this."

"You're telling me my business, lass?"

"I'm not telling you anything. I'm making a suggestion. And while I'm at it, I'd like to strongly suggest you stop calling me lass. My name, in case you've forgotten, is Samantha." She couldn't ask him to call her Ms. Wilde. Not after she'd seen him naked. Besides, the less he knew about her, the better.

He turned his attention to the job at hand without another word. Whether or not he was willing to admit it, Sam knew the elements were conspiring against them.

What was it they'd told her at her fear of flying classes? Deep thinking, deep talking—deep breathing, that was it. Deep, calming breaths just like pregnant women learned at Lamaze classes. Not that Sam believed a few deep breaths could quell either her fear of flying or the rigors of childbirth, but she might as well give it a try. She pulled air into her lungs, held it for a few seconds, then slowly released it. Then she did it again, more loudly this time.

He glanced at her over his shoulder. "You said something?"

Once again her face flamed. "No," she said. "Not a word." Hard to believe that back home she was considered unflappable.

"I heard something."

"It wasn't me." He probably didn't believe her, but that was his problem. Right now she had to concentrate all of her energy on the takeoff. It wasn't that she was superstitious or anything, but she knew that if she so much as blinked and lost concentration, something terrible would happen and—

A huge gust of wind slammed into the aircraft broadside and, muttering a curse, the pilot brought the plane to a screeching halt.

"I told you so." The words popped out before she had the chance to think about what she was saying. Terror will do that to a woman.

He unbuckled his seat belt, then stood up and faced her. He towered over her. His wide shoulders seemed to block out all light. For the first time she wasn't thinking about the way he'd looked naked. She was thinking about the way he'd look when he pleaded temporary insanity after they charged him with her murder.

"Take heed, lass." His voice was a controlled roar. "Say no more until we're up or I won't be held accountable."

"Up?" Her voice rose to match the word. "Are you crazy? How much more of a warning do you need?" She knew she was playing with fire but he was the one who'd lit the match.

"The winds shifted. There is no cause for alarm."

"That wind almost blew us halfway to Glasgow."

"We were in no danger. I've been flying for twenty years without incident."

"There's always a first time."

"Aye," he said darkly as he sat down. "For many things."

"You know what," she said, unbuckling her seat belt. "I think maybe I should find myself another pilot to take me to Stewart's castle." Even if it meant she had to spend the night in a deserted airport. There was something too driven about this man, too determined to buck the odds, for her taste.

The plane lurched forward once again.

"I don't have a good feeling about this," she said, moving toward the cockpit. "Stop so I can—"

"Too late," he said as the plane gathered speed.

"We haven't taken off yet. Just stop and I'll—"

The nose tilted upward and they were airborne.

"What on earth is the matter with you?" she demanded. "Have you lost your mind?"

"If you want to get to Glenraven, lassie, then this is the way to do it."

The plane's engine whined as the pilot urged it to climb higher and faster through the dark, menacing clouds. She'd been aboard jumbo jets that took a beating going through clouds like these. What chance would they have in this little bucket of bolts?

The plane trembled then bucked violently as they broke out of the clouds, and a small whimper of alarm escaped her lips.

"You'd better sit down, lass."

"I'm fine," she said as she pressed her eyes tightly closed. "I know all about CAT."

"Do you now?"

The plane shimmied, and she forced cool air into her lungs. "Clear air turbulence," she said. "It's nothing to worry about. It just feels like you're in trouble even though you're not."

"And where did you learn this fact?"

"My fear of flying class."

His laugh was wonderful. Dark and rich and genuine. She hated those fake laughs she heard sometimes in the boardroom of Wilde & Daughters Ltd. This man had the kind of laugh that took you by surprise and made you want to hear it again.

The plane dropped a few feet, steadied, then dropped again.

"Oh, my God—"

"Sit down," he ordered, pointing to the seat next to him.

"I'll sit down when I'm ready to sit down," she said, wondering how she was going to make it to the seat she'd abandoned. Almost on cue, the plane reared like an unbroken horse.

"Ready now?" he asked.

"I think so." She sank down next to him and fastened the seat belt with trembling fingers. "Clear air turbulence never lasts long." She knew that she was babbling but it kept her mind off the fact that she was a mile above the earth in a plane that was roughly the size of her father's Caddy. "They used to tell us that in class to trick us into getting on the plane in the first place."

"They were right," he said in that mellow Scots voice of his. "Clear air turbulence is all bluster and no might."

"So I have nothing at all to worry about," she went on. "Another minute or two and it'll be clear sailing."

"Aye," he said, "clear sailing if I can restart the engine."

Chapter Two

"That's a joke, isn't it?" Sam asked, her eyes wide
with fear. "Please tell me you're joking."

"Ice in the carburetor. We most likely picked it up
in the cloud cover." He obviously didn't believe in
sugarcoating the truth.

"We shouldn't have taken off," she said. "I told
you the weather was too risky."

"Quiet," he ordered. "I need to think."

Thinking's good, she agreed silently. Especially if
he thought up a way out of this mess.

She clasped her hands together tightly and rested
them in her lap. Her right foot drummed a tattoo
against the floor of the plane. Rat-tat-tattattat. Rat-tat-
tattattat. She waited for her life to pass before her
eyes. That's what they said happened when a woman
was about to meet her Maker, a parade of First Com-
munions and first teeth, of best friends and forgotten
lovers, all marching before you in review as you got
ready to breathe your last.

So why was it the only thing Sam saw when she
closed her eyes was the way the pilot had looked in
the glorious altogether?

She saw his broad shoulders, the rippling muscles of his back, the powerful legs—

Good grief, what was wrong with her? She was a woman of substance. She prided herself on her serious nature, her attention to detail, her unwavering focus on the important things in life. She wasn't the kind of woman who made a habit of ogling naked men. She usually didn't even find them that attractive. All of that anatomical detail seemed a little excessive to her, as if nature had gone a tad overboard with the design.

A few years ago she'd attended a bachelorette party for an employee at one of those male strip clubs. She'd been downright shocked by the way her normally cool, calm and collected staff turned slack-jawed at the sight of the G-stringed dancers. There was something so calculated about the whole experience that it was about as erotically stimulating as a triple root canal. All around her, women stomped and cheered and practically drooled over those perfect specimens while Sam wished she'd brought a good stock report to read.

Wouldn't you know it? She finally figured out what all the fuss was about and now she'd never have the chance to act on it.

A cosmic joke, that's what it was. One giant gotcha before the lights went out for good.

She inhaled sharply as the nose dipped toward the cloud cover. It took her a second to realize the pilot was talking to her.

"...and so I had my fortune read when I was a young man at university," he said, manipulating various dials and levers in what seemed to Sam an alarmingly random fashion. "Did you ever have your fortune told?"

"I don't believe in that nonsense," she said, forcing herself to ignore the deep and utter silence from the engine. "No one can foretell the future."

"Sophie could."

Her left brow arched. "Sophie?"

"A dark beauty she was in her prime." He paid no attention to a horrible grinding noise on the left. Sam struggled to do the same. "All said she had the gift."

"The gift," Sam repeated.

"The gift," he said solemnly. "The veil between this world and the other was thin as smoke to Sophie. She knew all."

The engine clicked three times in quick succession then fell silent again. A bead of sweat formed on the pilot's right temple. That was the kind of thing you didn't see when you were safely ensconced in first class on a jumbo jet heading for L.A. She could go a long time before seeing it again.

Still, he was going out of his way to be kind to a total stranger who was on the verge of a nervous breakdown. Maybe he was right. If they talked, she wouldn't be able to think.

She forced her voice into the bright and cheerful range. "So tell me more about Sophie."

He met her eyes and she saw something that might have been gratitude. "To this day I don't know much about her, but she knew all there was to know about me." He paused a beat. "More even than you, lassie."

The image of him, stark naked and glorious, rose

once again before her, and her entire body was suffused with sudden heat. "I'm sorry. I should have let you know I was standing there."

He grinned and she found herself grinning back at him, despite her fear. "No harm done, lass. Looking's not a crime."

"Now you tell me," she murmured. "You were talking about Sophie...."

He tried the engine again, and again nothing happened. A second bead of sweat joined the first. "She knew I was the one who broke the parson's window on Easter Sunday."

"And I suppose she told everyone."

"Worse," he said. "She held it over my head, the sorceress did. Made me weed her garden every day until the first frost as punishment, she did."

"A witch," Sam agreed as he twisted another set of dials. *Please, God,* she thought. *Please, please!*

"And myself so young and innocent." The engine came within a hairbreadth of catching but failed once more.

"What else did she see?" Sam asked. Fire, flood, famine...plane crashes.

"She saw a long and happy life."

"Can you trust her?"

"Ask me again in thirty seconds."

She didn't have to. His words were drowned out by the wonderful, welcome whine and rattle of the plane's engine as it finally kicked in. The nose angled up and they rose through the rain, above the treetops, and bounced their way through the clouds.

"You can breathe again," he said. The relief in his voice was unmistakable.

"I'm trying to but my lungs won't cooperate." She swiveled in her seat and looked at him. "Was it as close as I think it was?"

"Aye," he said, "and closer."

His face was in profile. The large proud head. Strong jaw. Straight nose. Lashes long and thick enough to make a woman weep with envy. She felt a fluttering in the pit of her belly and turned away.

"What brings you to Stewart's castle?" the pilot asked after a few minutes of silence.

She considered lying to him but thought better of it. "Business," she said.

"Not romance?"

"From what I've heard, Mr. Stewart isn't looking for love. A gallery owner in Glasgow told me he never leaves the castle."

"And who else did you talk to?"

"A banker in Edinburgh, a collector just outside St. Andrews. Believe me, there are lots of stories out there about the elusive Mr. Stewart." A thought occurred to her. "You said you know everyone in Loch Glenraven. That must mean you know Stewart."

"Our paths have crossed," the pilot said carefully.

She waited for him to say more and when he didn't, she prodded, "So what's he like? Did you ever fly him anyplace? Have you ever been inside the castle? Is he young, old, somewhere in between?"

"You ask too many questions, lass. Best you find out on your own."

"Would you introduce me to him?" It would save her the trouble of scaling the castle walls.

"I canna do that. The people of Glenraven respect

each other's privacy. I'd do nothing to betray any one of them.''

Tall, dark and honorable. It was a good thing Sam was the practical type. If she was the least bit romantic, she'd be half in love with him by now.

SO THEY WERE TALKING about him in Glasgow and Edinburgh, were they? Duncan Stewart hid his dissatisfaction behind the business of flying a plane. They were there to display and sell his work, not spread gossip from the Borders to the Highlands. He revealed his heart in his work. That should be enough for the vultures.

But it wasn't. They wanted the hows and the whys of each piece he sculpted, wanted them so badly they were willing to dig into the layers of his past to find them. But no matter how hard they tried to find his castle, no one had managed to until now.

"And who was it who told you about Glenraven?" he asked. "The Edinburgh banker or the St. Andrews collector?" He'd trusted them all.

"Neither one, actually." She had an easy way of talking that made every word sound the gospel truth. He pitied the man who loved her. One look into those clear blue eyes and he would believe the world was flat if she told him it was so. He was immune to that now and glad for it. "I figured that out myself, but I wasn't certain until you confirmed it."

And damn him for the fool he was. She'd worked some manner of sorcery on him. He wasn't one to let down his guard that easily.

"That doesn't explain it, lassie," he persisted. "You narrowed it down to Glenraven on your own?"

"Serendipity," she said, her drawl sliding up and down the word. She told him how she'd bought some newspapers at a kiosk in Glasgow and by chance happened onto a story about the Glenraven library. One of his earliest works, uncredited, was on display in the lobby, and she had recognized it as a Stewart at once, despite the grainy black-and-white newspaper photo.

It occurred to Duncan that he could save them both a great deal of time and effort if he told her who he was and why she was on a fool's errand, but she was so lovely, so animated as she told him of her plans, that he couldn't seem to find the words.

SAM WAS in midsentence when she realized the pilot was no longer listening to her. The look on his face made her blood run cold. "What's wrong?" she asked, her heart pumping harder. "Is it the carburetor again? More ice? You can handle that, right? Ice isn't a big problem, is it? You know how to handle it, right?"

"The electrical system is out," he said, his words clipped. "I canna get a reading on anything."

"The engine's still running, isn't it?" The engine had to be working. She didn't even want to think of what it might mean if it wasn't.

"We have nothing, lass."

"Nothing? We can't have nothing. We have to have something. If we don't have anything that means—"

His expression was grim. "We'll glide to a landing on the other side of this mountain. We have no other option."

"Glide to a landing on the other side of the mountain! You can't even *see* the mountain." She leaned as far forward as the seat belt would allow and peered out the window. All she saw was dense, icy fog, swirling everywhere.

"'Tis there, lass. Of that I'm certain."

"And you think we'll sail right over it and glide to a landing on the other side." Did he also believe in the tooth fairy and Santa Claus?

He grunted something she assumed meant yes.

"Is there an airport on the other side of this mountain?"

"I wish I could tell you there was, but I'd be a liar."

"I wouldn't mind a lie right about now."

If he got the joke, he didn't smile. Her stomach twisted into a sailor's knot.

"You're in the Highlands. The best we can hope for is some open land with room enough."

She'd seen enough of the Scottish terrain to know that what he was hoping for was a miracle. The Highlands weren't Texas. The odds of finding a flat, treeless plain were about a hundred to one.

The sailor's knot in her stomach tightened.

The nose of the plane dipped into the top of an icy gray cloud. The cabin began to shake, as if gripped by a giant unseen hand. Her eyes filled with tears.

"Don't cry, girl," he said gently. "All is not lost."

"I'm not crying," she managed to say, determined to ignore the fact that she was lying through her teeth.

"You have no need to worry," he went on in that whiskey-and-honey voice. "It can't be my time yet. The beautiful Sophie saw me surrounded by children with a loving woman by my side, and none of that has yet come to pass."

"I hope Sophie was right," she said, closing her eyes as they dived deeper into the cloud cover in their glide toward earth. Random thoughts and disjointed images played leapfrog inside her head. Words of love from a man of strength and character, a lapful of babies, the kind of life no one in her family had managed to achieve—all the things she'd told herself she didn't want or need suddenly rose up in front of her, beckoning her forward.

"You were right before," the pilot said as the plane angled down toward the mountain. "I should have listened to you and waited for the weather to pass us by."

"Don't give me too much credit." She forced a weak smile. "I'm a coward, remember? I would have advised the same thing during a spring shower." Careful, cautious Samantha Wilde, still waiting for her life to begin.

"There's nothing of the coward about you."

"If you knew me better, you wouldn't say that. I'm afraid of everything." Planes and snakes and marriage, and that was just for starters.

"Maybe," he allowed, "but nothing stops you."

"Now you're sounding like your friend Sophie. Unless you're psychic, you couldn't possibly know that."

"I know what I see, and I see you here next to me despite your fears."

"Maybe I'm crazy," she said, feeling her carefully constructed defenses being to crumble.

"Or passionate." He said the word the way it was

meant to be said, all sibilance and heat. Too bad it had about as much to do with her as moon rocks.

"Nobody has ever called me passionate before." Not even her former fiancé, John Singleton Reilly, which was one of the reasons he was her former fiancé. "I'm the practical one in the family."

"Practical women don't chase a man all the way to the Highlands."

"I've never chased a man in my life." She fairly bristled with indignation.

"You're chasing one now."

"It's not the way you make it sound."

"And how do I make it sound?"

"Like—" She hesitated, then decided to hell with it. In a few more minutes, none of this would matter any longer. They'd either be dead or so happy that neither would even remember this idiotic conversation. "Like I'm looking for a lover."

"Are you?"

"Absolutely not." She cleared her throat and tried again. "*Definitely* not."

"I heard you the first time."

"I wanted to make sure."

He glanced at her hands, which were clasped tightly in her lap. "No rings."

"I don't wear jewelry other than a watch," she said. Jewelry held none of the magical appeal for her that it did for most women. To her, it was just the family business.

"Is there a man in your life?"

"There was," she said after a moment, "but John found someone else." Her own words caught her by surprise. "You're the first person I've told that to.

The rest of my family thinks I broke the engagement because I love my work more than I loved John.'' She laughed quietly, as much a sigh as anything else. "Too bad John thought so, too.''

"And was he right about that?''

"Oh, yes.'' She couldn't stop the words if she wanted to. "Poor John got out while the getting was good. He married his little girlfriend and they're expecting a baby. And I have my work.''

A dark silence fell across them. Normally she sought to fill silences with empty words, taking on all the silences in the world as if they were somehow her fault. This time she let it be.

It had felt good, telling her secret. She'd carried it around with her for so long now that it had acquired power over her it didn't deserve. All these months and she'd been unable to tell her sisters or her father, and now, in the blink of an eye, she'd unburdened her heart on a stranger.

The pilot wasn't her friend or her lover. He wasn't anything to her at all, and somehow that fact seemed to lower the rest of her defenses.

"It's not like I'm obsessed or anything. I know the difference between work and play, but it seems like I'm the only one in the family who understands that I do. My father has suddenly turned into a combination of dictator and matchmaker, my sister Martie is getting married, and my other sister Frankie is playing beachcomber on Maui. We're hemorrhaging profits on a daily basis and if we don't do something fast, we'll have to sell out to one of those horrid jewelry store chains you see in the malls.''

"What has this to do with Duncan Stewart?''

"Isn't it crystal clear? We've lost our edge and it's showing in the bottom line. We need something—or someone—to propel us into the next century, and I think he's the one who can do it.'' His genius, the raw erotic power of his sculptures, had cast their spell over Sam, and she knew deep in her gut that could translate into spectacular jewelry.

"You think he'll design for you?"

"I don't know," she said honestly. "All I know is that from the moment I first saw his work in a magazine, I knew I had to find him."

"Sex," he said in a voice that betrayed no particular emotion. "The engine that powers the world."

"There's that," she said, not dodging the issue, "but it's his loneliness that speaks louder to me."

"His loneliness?" he asked. "From the things written about him, you wouldn't think he had time to be lonely."

"I haven't read those stories," she said honestly. "All I know about him is what I see in his work, and I know he's right for Wilde & Daughters."

"Passion," he said again, more slowly this time. "You canna deny it, lassie."

She opened her mouth to read him a laundry list of her shortcomings, then stopped. Was it possible that he was right? She fought like a lion for what she believed in, whether it was a new direction for Wilde & Daughters Ltd. or the right to live her life the way she wanted to live it, despite her father's intervention. "Passionate." Her smile widened, despite the situation. "I like that."

"Hold that thought," he said. "The mountain lies just ahead."

As if on cue, the fog parted and a heavily wooded patch of mountainside appeared below them.

"We're going to make it!" she cried, her usual inhibitions vanishing. "We'll clear the mountain with room to spare."

"Not so fast," he said, and she noted the vein pulsing at his temple. "We're not there yet."

More of the fog parted, revealing more of the mountainside. And that mountainside was dead ahead.

A bead of sweat eased down the back of her neck and slid under the collar of her blouse. "You can do it," she said, as much to herself as to the man beside her. "You did it before. You brought the engine back to life. What's a little mountain?"

HER WORDS came to him through the rush of blood pounding in his ears. The words themselves didn't matter to him, but the sweet sound of her voice—that was everything. He focused on her voice like the North Star, hung his hopes and prayers on the rise and fall of it, those round vowels and gentle consonants drifting toward him on the wind of dreams.

Because it was a dream. All of it. This bloody thing they called life was a construct of imagination and hope, and it was about to be ripped from them in a few seconds unless they happened upon a miracle. And, in his experience, miracles were in short supply. There hadn't been a miracle come his way to save his child or his marriage. He had no reason to think a miracle would find him now.

But she kept talking to him, putting aside her own fears, giving him a reason to keep hoping in the face of doom. She'd seen past the heat and into the darkness. She'd seen into the heart he kept hidden away, the heart he was sure he had lost.

"We're almost there," she was saying. "You can do anything...you can do anything you need to do...."

He made what adjustments he could to the glide path, trying to slow the rate of descent, but gravity was calling them home.

"You can make it happen, I know you can...."

And he found himself believing her. He didn't need to wait for miracles, he would make this miracle happen himself.

"The two of us," he heard himself saying. "We can do it together."

"Yes," she said. "The two of us, we can do it. Look!" Her voice rose with excitement. "A clearing! Just beyond the stream."

He saw it just where she pointed. All they had to do was cross the boulder-choked stream and one hundred yards of empty space lay waiting for them. He made rapid mental calculations of distance and speed and the pull of gravity. He made quick adjustments to the few cable-driven mechanisms at his disposal.

Then he met her eyes and in their beautiful blue depths he saw nothing but confidence in him. He didn't know where it came from or how he came to deserve it, but there it was, and he knew he would fashion her a miracle.

"Hold tight, lass." He gripped the wheel and held it steady as the plane skimmed the tops of the trees.

"Almost there," she whispered, "almost there."

The stream was wider than he'd expected. Jagged rocks and tumbling water. Certain disaster if they touched down near its banks. The nose of the plane dipped lower still, and for a moment he thought they were going to pitch forward and free-fall the rest of the way, but a friendly tailwind seemed to lift the small craft, cradling it just long enough to clear the stream.

A little more...a little more... They were so close to a miracle. Luck was with them. It had to be.

SAM HELD HER BREATH as they skimmed the stream. Rocks jutted up from the water, ready to pierce the fragile skin of the plane or pierce the gas tank. The pilot pulled back hard on the wheel then turned it to the right and the plane moved almost imperceptibly in that direction.

"Almost," she said in a long exhale of breath. "Almost there." As long as they both believed that, everything would be all right.

She heard the long scrape of rock against the little plane's belly, followed by a ripping sound and the harsh clank of metal folding in on itself. They bounced their way across the rough ground, nearly tilting end over end. Her elbow slammed against the instrument panel. The pain shot straight into her skull. The left wing caught in the branches of a dead bramble bush. The plane skidded sideways, swung around on itself, then stopped cold.

The silence was deeper than the grave. For a second she wondered if they were dead, but his words broke the quiet.

"Unbuckle, lass," he ordered, releasing his seat belt and standing up. "The tank is almost empty, but I still think it will blow."

Her hands shook so hard she couldn't manage the simple task. The sharp stink of petrol seared her nostrils.

"Hurry," he ordered, grabbing a black bag from behind his seat.

"I'm trying," she said, practically in tears. "I can't seem to—" Her fingers seemed like huge and unwieldy pieces of deadwood.

He bent in front of her and unfastened the belt.

"Now, lassie! We haven't much time."

He reached for her hand.

She hesitated for an instant, then took it.

The connection between them seemed as strong as life itself.

Together they leaped from the plane and ran toward a stand of trees a few hundred yards away. He pulled her behind an outcropping of rock, and a second later an explosion echoed through the silent clearing and the small plane went up in flames.

Chapter Three

They stared at the plane and then at each other and started to laugh.

"You did it!" she cried, throwing back her head and tossing the triumphant words to the sky. "I knew you could!"

Adrenaline pumped through his veins. He felt like he could throw a rope around the moon and reel it in. "We did it together, lassie," he said, pulling her close to him. "'Twas you who kept me going."

Her cheeks were flushed with excitement. Her sleek fall of pale blond hair was tousled, drifting over her right eye, curving across her cheek. He wondered suddenly how he'd lived so long without her in his sight. Or had she always been there, hidden inside his heart?

"I didn't do anything," she said, her gaze locked on his. "You deserve all the credit."

He held her flower of a face between his hands. He wanted to inhale her, breathe her essence right into his very soul.

Sam wanted to wrap herself around him and never let go. The feel of his big strong body against hers, the way he was looking into her eyes, as if he could see all the way to her secret soul. She was alive to him, more alive than she'd ever been before, so alive that her skin registered his presence.

Magic was everywhere, in the way he sounded and looked and the way he made her feel. They'd faced death together and lived to tell the tale. That did something to a woman. She was pure sensation. The wall of glass that surrounded her heart had shattered, leaving her vulnerable and hungry.

Kiss me, she thought. She wanted to feel his mouth against hers, that delicious pressure, she wanted to know how he would taste and smell and sound. She wanted to know she was alive in every way possible before the real world rushed in again and reminded her that she was cautious, careful Samantha Wilde who didn't want anything at all.

Duncan knew what she was thinking. Not the words—he couldn't know the words—but the intent. A man would have to be blind to miss the look in her eyes. Or was it his own aching, empty need reflected back? He didn't know, but somehow it didn't seem to matter. Only touch mattered. The way she fit against him.

He dipped his head toward hers.

She lifted her face toward his.

If he hesitated, she would break away.

If she lowered her eyes, he would understand.

The moment between them seemed to stretch like a length of golden cord, winding itself around their hearts until there was nothing else they could do but the one thing they'd been moving toward since the very first instant.

His mouth found hers—or was it she who did the

finding? Neither one knew or cared. There was in that instant such a powerful sense of connection, of destiny, that their minds were empty of all but the wonders to be found in a kiss.

Her mouth was silky and hot and sweet and he drank her in the way he drank a fine wine.

His lips were firm, unyielding, demanding responses from her that she had only dreamed about. He parted her lips with the tip of his tongue and all of her secret places came instantly to life. She was on fire from the inside out, a sweet liquid fire that she'd never known before.

She placed her hands against his chest, that rock-hard wall of muscle, and savored the feel of his heart beating beneath her palms.

He let his hands slide slowly from her face to the delicate column of her throat, until his thumbs found the wild-bird pulsing at the base. Then, so slowly, he moved down over her collarbone, down, down, until he cupped her breasts with his palms. Small and firm and warm—and perfect. So perfect it made him ache with wanting her.

Her eyes fluttered closed. She was drunk on sensation. The sight of him. The feel of him. The way he was touching her, with hunger and awe, reverence and heat. Did he know—could he possibly imagine—what he was doing to her? She wanted to feel his hands on every part of her body, breasts and belly and between her legs.

His hands slid over her rib cage then spanned her waist. Her hips were narrow, her flat belly quivered when he rested his hands upon it and he grew rock hard in response. She moved against him then, her body arching against his as small sounds of pleasure seemed to fill his brain. Her thighs were long and lean beneath the prim skirt. He began to inch her skirt up over those glorious thighs, revealing their shape and line to his eyes. He laughed, low and delighted, when he reached the lacy band midway up.

"A garter belt, lassie?"

She buried her face against his shoulder in embarrassment but she didn't move away from his touch. She couldn't even if she wanted to. That touch was life itself.

Her cotton panties surprised him. A strange counterpoint to the eroticism of the garter belt, but he was beginning to understand she was a woman of contradictions. He wanted to learn every one. His fingers played with the soft material, registering the wet heat of her body burning through it, then he pushed the garment over her hips and began a slow exploration of her honeyed secrets.

Her knees buckled at the touch of his fingers against the delicate folds of flesh. Nothing was the way she remembered it, not this sleek, gliding arousal, the flood of warmth between her thighs, not the empty place inside her that ached to be filled by only this one man.

He was strong enough, hard enough, ready enough for both of them. Gripping her hips, he lifted her and urged her to wrap her legs around his waist. The feel of those lithely muscled thighs came close to unmanning him.

She trembled with need as he slowly lowered her onto his erection. It had been so long...it had been forever. Nothing in her life had prepared her for the sheer exhilaration of surrender. No thoughts. No worries. Only wave after wave of wild sensation meant to send her spinning above the clouds. She felt her body close itself around him and she urged him deeper, rode him harder, wanted to draw him toward the center of her being and into her heart.

And that was where he wanted, needed to be. This was about possession of the most primal sort, about claiming a mate, about finding that missing piece of yourself, the piece you'd spent your life searching for.

They came together in a violent, soul-shattering climax that left them panting and spent and still hungry for each other. He found shelter for them beneath a stand of small pines. He opened the emergency kit and spread one of the two insulating blankets out on the bed of fragrant needles, then lay her gently down with only the other thin silvery blanket to shield them from the wind and the rain. And then he made love to her again.

Slowly.

Thoroughly.

Discovering how she looked as well as how she felt.

Discovering how she tasted on his tongue.

Wondering how he would ever let her go now that he'd found her.

Sam felt as if she was suspended in a dream as he worked his magic. No man had ever done that for her before. She probably wouldn't have allowed it if they'd tried. She couldn't have imagined opening herself to anyone quite that way, in either body or soul. To be so vulnerable, so trusting, so openly, blatantly needy for what a man could give to her.

For the way this man could make her feel.

This had to be a dream. Nothing else could explain it. Wasn't she the woman who didn't need anything but her work? The woman who thought of nothing but the company that had been family and friend and lover to her for as long as she could remember.

Of course it was a dream. And since it was a dream, she could give herself up to the sweet, pure pleasure of it for as long as it lasted.

SAM WOKE UP to the sound of a car engine in the distance. She was curled in the pilot's arms, both of them sheltered beneath the pine trees, both of them cozy beneath his insulating blanket. She felt warm, satisfied and not quite ready to be rescued.

But, like it or not, rescue was at hand.

She leaned over and pressed a kiss to the side of her Scotsman's jaw. "Better wake up," she whispered. "We have company."

He mumbled something, then flung an arm across his eyes.

An odd feeling blossomed inside her chest as she looked at him. What was it about a sleeping man, anyway, that turned a woman to mush? She'd seen her ex-fiancé asleep many times—at the opera and the movies, for starters—and the sight had done nothing but annoy her. With this man, however, it was another story.

"So sleep a little longer," she said, rising to her feet. "I'll greet our visitors." From the sound of the engine, they'd be here any minute, and the last thing she wanted was for them to know what she and the pilot had been doing.

Unfortunately, her bags with all her toiletries had gone up with the plane. She dragged her fingers through her hair in an attempt to restore a semblance of style, but to no avail. The pilot's emergency kit rested a few feet away. She hesitated—it wasn't her bag, after all—then decided he probably wouldn't mind if she searched through it for a comb.

After all they'd shared, how could he possibly object to sharing a piece of plastic with her?

She unzipped one side of the bag then reached in. Flashlight. Flares. Another, smaller bag. She pulled it out, unsnapped the flap, then peeked inside. Success! She grabbed a comb and was about to replace the smaller bag in the larger one when she noticed a badge of some kind. Her curiosity got the better of her and she plucked it out. The picture was the usual ID-style snapshot, but not even bad photography could dim the subject's good looks. Her Scotsman was one gorgeous specimen. Her gaze flickered over a string of license numbers, hair color, eye color, name—

Duncan Fraser Stewart.

She blinked then looked again.

Duncan Fraser Stewart.

"Oh, my God," she breathed, as the blood seemed to rush down to her feet. This couldn't be happening. The man she'd made mad, passionate love to couldn't possibly be the same man she'd traveled to Scotland to find. The reclusive artist, the genius, the man who was going to save Wilde & Daughters Ltd.

She looked at his sleeping form. That body she now knew as well as she knew her own—the thought made her feel light-headed with a combination of shame and anger. She wanted to hit him over the head with the emergency kit then tell him what a no-good, rotten son of a—

She caught herself. If she did that, she'd have to face him, and that was the one thing she didn't think she could do. Murder him, yes. Talk to him? Not on your life.

She heard the sound of an engine idling nearby then a voice called out, "Hallo? Who's there?"

The thought of enduring a ride to the nearest village with that rat Stewart was more than she could contemplate.

She looked at him again. He was still deeply asleep. If he'd heard their rescuer call out, he gave no indication.

"Get up," she said, in as quiet a voice as she could manage. "We have company."

He didn't so much as move a muscle.

What a shame.

Nobody could say she hadn't tried.

Turning, she went to head their rescuer off at the pass.

With a little luck, Duncan Stewart would wake up alone.

With a lot of luck, he'd spend the rest of his life that way.

Glenraven Castle, six weeks later

"Up all night he is," Old Mag said to Robby, the caretaker. "Don't work at all, just drowns himself in whiskey and howls at the moon."

"'Tis a lass, plain and simple." Robby poured

himself a cup of tea from the blue china pot that sat in the middle of the kitchen table. "This is how it was the first time."

"Och!" Old Mag shot him her fiercest look. "Mention that one's name in this house, man, and deal with my wrath."

"The devil take her," Robby agreed. "Her name will never pass these lips again."

"Broke his heart, the witch." Mag poured herself three fingers of single malt from a half-empty bottle. "He's never been the same."

"Aye," Robby said, "until now. I'm a man, Mag, and I know what I know. There's a new lass. He fights his heart now, but it's a losing battle."

"Have you two nothing better to do?" Duncan Stewart roared as he strode into the kitchen. He'd heard enough of the conversation to know it was time to put a stop to it. "Do I pay you to sit here and talk about me?"

"And the pay not nearly enough," Mag muttered, glaring at him. She'd been part of the family since he was a wee bairn and knew how far she could push. "You should be taking care of your own business, not minding ours."

Duncan ignored the comment. If he engaged the old woman in battle, they'd be at it until sunup. "I'm going into town," he announced. "More than that no one needs to know."

Mag and Robby exchanged a look.

"Say no more," he warned. "There are young ones in need of employment who'd be willing to do your jobs for half the wages."

Mag snorted. "Aye," she said, "and wouldn't you

be the one, looking to save a tuppence on the back of an old woman."

"You'll outlive us all," Duncan said. Two minutes with Old Mag and he sounded more Scottish than Robert the Bruce.

"God willin'," said Robby.

"God willin'," said Mag and Duncan.

"And what would I tell a body if he calls?"

Duncan threw his hands up in exasperation. "Tell him what you like, old woman," he bellowed. "I'm past caring."

He stormed out, striding past the north turret that served as his studio. Old Mag and Robby had known him all his life. They were more his parents than his own parents had been. It was Old Mag who'd wiped away his tears when he skinned a knee and Robby who'd taught him the things a young boy needed to know to make his way in the world. His own parents were perfectly nice people, but the world of childhood had been beyond their understanding. By the time Duncan was a man, the gap between them had grown too wide to bridge.

His father was gone now, ten years dead and buried. His mother had followed a year ago Christmas.

And Duncan was still alone.

Years ago, when he was young and idealistic, he thought he'd found the woman he would grow old with. He'd met Lana at university, when he was a struggling art student and she was an artist's model with her eye on a stage career. He had been captivated by her dark eyes, her catlike face, her tiny body with the surprising curves. She had been captivated by his castle and all that came with it. It had taken him four years of marriage—and one tragedy—before he understood that simple fact.

His Highland heritage had served him well. When grief threatened to pull him under, he withdrew to the castle and poured his emotions into his work. And it was his work that saved him.

And no one had ever recognized the loneliness at the core of everything he did. Nobody until Samantha.

The beautiful American had awakened something in him he'd thought long dead. He might not have shared his identity with her but he had shared his heart, and look what she'd done in return—set the hounds of Fleet Street on his heels. She'd apparently returned to Glasgow and made certain that every reporter in the city knew she'd left Duncan Stewart stranded by his wrecked Cessna alongside Loch Glenraven.

Artist in Plane Crash, read one of the headlines. His face was in the newspapers, and so was his whole sordid story. His failed marriage to Lana, his castle, his solitary state of mind—everything except the thing that meant the most to him in the world, his work. They brushed over his finest sculptures in a half sentence, then devoted endless paragraphs to speculating about the American woman who'd been in the plane crash with him.

Even Lana had been interviewed on movie location in Africa. She hadn't said much but had cleverly managed to mention the name of her newest film at least three times. She was as beautiful and cruel as ever, the woman he'd loved once. Lana had married two more times since their divorce and was about to try for number four. He marveled at her optimism. He had none left. She had made certain of that when she left.

The American lass did him a favor, he thought, as he climbed into the Land Rover he kept parked behind the stables. They'd been naked in soul and body that afternoon by the lake. He would have told her everything if she'd stayed with him, would have offered up his heart—or at least what little heart he had to offer. He supposed he should be grateful because, by walking out on him the way she did, she'd saved him from making another mistake.

Houston, Texas, that same day

"YOU DON'T have to snap my head off, Ms. Wilde." Jack, her administrative assistant, faced her across her desk. "You've been in a bad mood since you came home from that mystery trip, and I'm tired of taking the blame."

Samantha looked up from a stack of papers a foot high. "What was that, Jack?" she asked. Lately she seemed to be having a terrible time concentrating. No matter what she was doing, no matter how hard she tried, all thoughts led to Duncan Stewart.

Jack gave her a baleful look then turned and left her office. He'd get over it, whatever it was. People always did. Anger vanished. Annoyance faded. Even lust cooled.

Or at least she hoped it did. She only thought about Duncan Stewart eight or ten times a day now, instead of a dozen times an hour. Progress, she told herself. Definitely progress.

She'd just gone over third-quarter projections for

Wilde & Daughters Ltd. and the prognosis was grim. Her sister Martie was one of the best jewelry designers in the country, but jewelry wasn't enough. Not if the company was going to survive. Besides, Martie was getting married soon and heading off on her honeymoon. Who knew what would happen once her little sister got a taste of domestic life? What if she got pregnant and decided she'd rather change diapers than dream up new and exotic jewelry designs for the rich and privileged?

Marriage did strange things to people. Her parents' Byzantine marital histories were proof of that.

The company needed to go in a new direction, and she'd been dead certain Duncan Stewart was the creative genius who could take them there. Now she'd never have the chance to find out if she'd been right.

Never mix business and great sex. Isn't that what they'd taught her at Harvard Business School? If they hadn't, they should have. The moment a woman let down her guard and became a woman, the game was over. At least when it came to the dollars-and-cents business of making money. She'd lost her advantage with the first kiss, and now she could never get it back.

She leaned back in her chair and closed her eyes. It seemed like she hadn't had a decent night's sleep in years. Since her return from Scotland, she felt as if she were operating underwater, moving through her day in a hazy kind of slow motion that made her feel out of sync with the entire universe.

She'd thought she was doing a pretty good job of covering up, but apparently she was wrong. Her father, Lucky, his assistant, Estelle, even her about-to-be-married sister, Martie, had all commented on the circles under her eyes and her shortness of temper. "Thanks," she'd growled at Martie just yesterday. "Next time you have a bad hair day, I'll be sure to point it out."

And now Jack told her she'd been in a bad mood since her mystery trip.

She tried to tell herself it was spring fever, but it was already mid-June, with summer right around the corner.

Tears burned behind her lids but she'd be darned if she would let them fall. If she gave in to tears for even a second, she'd be lost. Her emotions were right there at the surface, and it took every ounce of strength to keep them from getting the better of her. The most bizarre things made her cry—garbage bag commercials on television, rock videos, the theme song from *Friends*. Last week she'd even picked up the telephone and called her mother in London.

Julia had sounded her usual self, glad to hear from Sam but not particularly curious about the details of her daughter's life. Julia prattled on about the wonderful play she'd seen and the marvelous man who was taking her to dinner that night and never once asked Sam why she'd called. By the time Sam hung up, she felt worse than ever. All weepy and wishing she could have had a mother instead of a pal. She would never do that to a child, blur the lines between them. She would never abandon a child to grow up without her. And then she wondered why she was thinking about any of this when having a baby was the furthest thing from her mind.

She was either suffering from post-traumatic stress disorder or losing her mind.

This was what happened when you let your heart rule your head. Cool, controlled Samantha finally threw caution to the wind and ended up sleeping with the man she'd wanted to impress with her business acumen and not her bedroom skills. There was definitely a lesson to be learned from the experience, and as soon as she forgot the way she'd felt in his arms, she'd figure out what it was.

Glasgow

"WE CAN DELIVER a new plane to you by Friday next, Mr. Stewart," said the salesman to Duncan later that afternoon.

"That's the best you can do?"

The young man nodded. "I'm afraid so."

"Then so be it," said Duncan, signing his check. "Ring me when it's delivered and I'll drive down."

They shook hands and Duncan left the sales office. At least he'd accomplished one thing today. He felt about his plane the way American movie cowboys felt about their horses, and he was lost without it. Fleet Street's interest in his crash—and the subsequent resurrection of interest in his personal life—had finally waned, and he'd ventured to Glasgow to see about reclaiming his life.

The long drive down from Loch Glenraven had given him time to think. He hadn't done much thinking at the castle, but not for want of trying. The good citizens of Glenraven had banded together to keep the gossips and the press at bay. They knew nothing.

They said nothing. They offered nothing in the way of comfort for the throngs of reporters. It didn't take long for the city folk to fold up their tents and leave.

And then there was Old Mag, who watched his every move and commented on each one of them. "Something happened to you," she'd said, "and I'll find out what. Mark me well on that, laddie."

So he'd spent much of the past six weeks barricaded in his studio, trying to lose himself in his work, but no matter what he tried—clay or marble or wood—the result was always the same. His beautiful American was everywhere, in everything he did, every word he uttered, every thought that rose half formed from his heart.

And he didn't want her there.

He tried to drown the image of her in whiskey but she would not be denied. He hadn't planned to make love to her. They'd faced death and lived to tell the tale. What happened between them afterward had been as inevitable as drawing their next breaths, a celebration of life. Only a fool would read more into the interlude than that.

That sense of destiny, of something beyond the moment, had been a product of his own imagining.

He climbed into his Land Rover and started the engine. The road to Glenraven was on the far side of Glasgow. He had noticed a pub not far from there where he could get a pint and some food to sustain him on the long drive to the castle.

He rarely came into the city. He hated the crowds and the noise of city life, hated the drab gray buildings and the smell of petrol in the air. The city diminished him. His wild and beautiful Highlands restored him. It was that simple.

"Sit where you like," the bartender called as he stepped into the dimly lit establishment a few minutes later. "We have stout if you're of a mind."

"Aye," said Duncan. "And soup and a loaf of bread while you're at it."

"A man after my own heart," said the bartender, laughing. "My Celia will bring it to you in a wink."

If the man recognized him from the newspaper stories, he gave no indication. For the first time in weeks, Duncan felt himself relax. He claimed one of the small tables and glanced around the pub. A stag's head decorated the far wall. Mounted fish lined the wall behind the bar. The other walls boasted a tartan plaque, an ad for Guinness and an oil painting of William Wallace, among other things.

"Your pint," said the bartender, placing the heavy glass before him. "And good health to you."

Duncan raised the glass in salute. The stout was dark and strong and it went down smooth as silk. He was glad he'd stopped here instead of at one of the fancy restaurants in Glasgow proper. A radio played softly in the background, some music, soccer scores, a man railing against the monarchy. There was something comforting about the mix of sights and sounds and smells.

This was his land. This was where he belonged.

Celia, a round woman in her early sixties, bustled up to him, bearing a tray overhead. "I hope pepper pot be to your liking." Her tone was brisk but friendly. "And this is the best honey-oatmeal bread in all of Scotland."

She placed a steaming bowl in front of him and a basket of bread still warm from the oven. He thanked her. She stood next to him, waiting.

He looked at her. "Is something wrong?" he asked.

"Eat," she said.

He ate a spoonful of soup.

"And?" she asked.

"Delicious," he said.

"The bread." She pointed to the basket. "Try it."

He took a bite, chewed, then swallowed. "The best."

Celia beamed with pleasure. "Finish," she said, "then I'll bring you more." She hurried to the kitchen.

"Forty-two years," the bartender said as the door closed behind Celia. He beamed with pride. "Six children and thirty-two grands."

Duncan met the man's eyes. "You have a lot to be thankful for."

"And don't I know that." He poured himself a whiskey then joined Duncan at his table. "A man's family is everything," he said. "Everything. Children are the reason we're born."

"I wouldn't know," said Duncan. "I have none."

The man looked sympathetic. "Our first bairn was six years coming."

"And I have no wife." Had he lost his mind then, telling all to a stranger?

"A man needs a wife," the bartender stated in a tone that left no room for discussion. "We're not meant to go through this life alone."

A few weeks ago Duncan would have argued the

man under the table. Now he was no longer sure. In one afternoon, she had seen through to his loneliness, to a place no one else on earth knew existed, and now he seemed trapped within the emptiness.

"I had a wife," Duncan said carefully, "but she wasn't one for family."

"Then you need a new one, man, and soon. You're not getting any younger."

"I have a good life," he said, "and work I care about."

"Ach," said the bartender with a look of disgust. "Work cannot warm your bed at night."

"A hot water bottle can warm my bed more efficiently," Duncan said. "What need do I have for a wife?"

The man waggled a finger in Duncan's direction. "You joke now, lad, but in twenty years you'll be wishing you'd listened to Gordon. I thought like you once. Thirty years I lived without my Celia, and happily, but from that first day I knew there was no life without her."

"Love at first sight? You must be reading women's books, old man."

Gordon ignored the remark. "She walked into the pub with her brother and ordered a cup of tea. 'And would you like whiskey with that?' I asked, and she gave me one of those looks that the lasses give and my heart was no longer mine." His expression softened with the memory. "We were wed three months later."

"A nice story," Duncan said, "but it has nothing to do with me."

"You have the look of one who's seen the light."

"I've the look of one who wants to eat his meal."

"And I'll leave you to it," said Gordon, rising to his feet. "You may be right at that, laddie. Some men are best left on their own."

Duncan ate the rest of his meal in silence. The pub was filled with people old and young, all of them happy and laughing and glad to be out and about on an evening in early summer.

They were all couples, he realized, looking about. Two by two like the animals on Noah's ark. He was the only one who sat alone and he wondered if it would always be that way.

The stout turned to sludge in his mouth and he tossed down his money and left the pub.

Houston

THE REALTOR had told Sam that the two-story town house would be a great investment. "Four percent per year, guaranteed," he'd coaxed before she decided to sign on the bottom line. "A little paint, some curtains, it'll be just like home."

That was three years ago. New paint and curtains had prettied up the place, but she was still waiting for it to feel like home.

She slipped on her bathrobe then padded downstairs to make a late supper. She'd stayed at the office until nearly nine o'clock, reworking facts and figures, delaying the moment when she entered the quiet apartment and closed the door behind her. Had it always been so deadly quiet in there or was she listening with new ears?

She switched on the tiny television set that was

suspended beneath one of the kitchen cabinets. *Seinfeld* was on. She listened absently to their banter while she made herself a bowl of cereal for dinner.

She'd planned to bring home Chinese food but the thought of that explosion of flavor made her queasy and she'd opted for cornflakes instead. In point of fact, she seemed to be queasy a lot lately. All sorts of things turned her stomach inside out—the smell of fresh paint, bacon sizzling, fountain pen ink. Actually she hadn't been right since she had the flu the week before leaving for Scotland.

She ate her cornflakes at the kitchen table while checking her To Do list. Martie's surprise bridal shower was tomorrow, and Sam had easily sixty high-priority items lined up and ready to go.

"I wish you'd bring someone with you, Sammy," her sister had said to her when she finalized the guest list. "What about Judd Simon? He seems like a nice man."

"Will you stop?" she'd pleaded with Martie. "If I wanted to bring someone to the wedding, I would, but I don't. I'll sit with Cousin Will during the reception." Will was a groomsman and would be her partner during the processional.

"Will's bringing a date," Martie said. "You'll be the only one there without one."

"Maybe it'll start a new trend," Sam said. "And, for your information, Estelle never brings a date anywhere."

"She is this time," Martie said smugly. "Deno Accardi from Accounting."

It was well-known around Wilde & Daughters Ltd. that Estelle Ross was head-over-heels in love with

Lucky. Estelle had worshipped the ground he walked on for as long as Sam could remember.

"I can't believe she'd bring a date when she could just grab a ride with Daddy." They'd be spending most of their time together, as always.

"I think she's trying to make him jealous," Martie said. "Maybe that will wake him up."

Sam had said nothing. Romantic strategy had always baffled her. Given his marital track record, why on earth would anyone want Lucky to try again? The odds were certainly against a happy ending.

But then why would her sister be so willing to leap into marriage? Martie and Trask had been separated for ten long years, the years that took Martie from girl to woman. Trask came back into her life and bam! One month later and they're walking down the aisle.

Martie and Trask were different people now, Sam thought. Adults with histories and needs and expectations. It was like marrying a stranger, and yet Martie glowed with a happiness and contentment that baffled Sam. Where did her sister get the optimism, the *courage,* to join her life with Trask's when she barely knew him? Certainly she didn't know the man he was now.

And yet it didn't seem to matter. When the heart told you it was right, all the cool logic in the world didn't stand a chance.

Her little sister understood that. Why couldn't Sam?

Chapter Four

Scotland

Old Mag stormed into Duncan's studio on the first morning of July.

He was standing by the window, nursing a tumbler of whiskey, when he heard the sound of her leather slippers against the tile floor.

"'Tis a crime the way you're behavin'," she railed in a tone of voice that dared him to argue. "Have you lost your mind or is this the way it is to be now?"

"You're daft, old woman," he said, pouring more single malt down his throat. "Nothing's changed."

The wagging finger brushed against his nose. "Keepin' secrets, that's what they say about you in town. That another bonny lass has broke your heart."

"As if a man could keep a secret in Glenraven," he said, looking at the fierce old woman who stood before him.

"Is it love, laddie, or hot blood?"

"I'll not answer that, you nosy crone."

The lines on Old Mag's road map of a face rearranged themselves into a smile. "'Tis love, I'd be thinking."

"You don't think," Duncan said, "or you wouldn't come to that conclusion."

"Love," Old Mag repeated. "Your fancy talk can't hide the truth from my old eyes."

"Not love," he said, more quietly this time then looked out the window. "Not love."

She placed a gnarled hand on his forearm and patted him. That hand had rocked his cradle and wiped away his tears. "'Tis my fondest wish that you find a lassie to love you true."

"In this world, Old Mag, I don't know if such a lass exists."

"Then look for her," Mag roared from the depths of her warrior's soul, "for she will not come lookin' for you."

DUNCAN TOLD HIMSELF he was flying to Glasgow on business that afternoon.

And when he could not find out what he needed to know in Glasgow, he told himself it was business that took him to St. Andrew's.

And from St. Andrew's to Edinburgh, to every dealer and collector his beautiful American might have questioned.

The Circadian Gallery was closed. Ronald Penwirth was in London for the week. Laura McVeigh of Renko's remembered meeting Samantha but hadn't bothered to get her name. "I told her nothing about you, Duncan," she said proudly. "Our clients' privacy is of paramount importance to us."

He went through every dealer and collector he

could think of until only Margaret Sinclair was left. Margaret had mounted one of his first shows and considered him her discovery. She was in her early eighties now, but still active in the art world.

"What a grand surprise!" Margaret greeted Duncan warmly with a kiss to both cheeks. "I wasn't expecting to see you again until the show in April. With the time you've been having, I thought you'd stay in the castle."

"I have a favor to ask of you, Margaret," he said. "You're the only one who can help me."

Margaret's lined face lit up with amusement. "Ach, lad, if only that were true. In my youth, I'd have met you measure for measure."

"And I'd have considered myself a lucky man."

"You can be a sweet talker, Duncan Stewart, when you've a mind to be." She took a sip of Scotch. "So tell me, what is it you're looking for?"

He met her eyes. "A woman."

Margaret's cheeks reddened and she laughed. "You're a bold one, make no mistake about it. Any particular woman?"

He pulled out a folded piece of paper then handed it to the woman. "Her name is Samantha. She's American, maybe from Texas. I drew this picture of her. If you've seen her—" He clipped the end of his sentence rather than betray himself any further.

Margaret smoothed out the paper as she studied the pencil study he'd sketched in the Land Rover. "This doesn't do her justice. She had lovely coloring—taffy blond hair and cornflower blue eyes."

He could hear his pulse beating in his ears. "Then you've seen her?"

"Aye." She folded the paper then handed it to him. "She came looking for you, laddie, the day of your crash, but I told her nothing. I would not help anyone invade your privacy."

"I know that, Margaret. She found me through her own means. It's her name I want."

"I do not remember her name," Margaret said. "And look at the face on you, my friend. I'll remind you not to kill the messenger. I do not remember her name but I do remember where I filed her business card." Her sweet expression darkened into a scowl as she flipped open a long wooden box and removed a card. "Is this the woman who turned the dogs of Fleet Street loose on you?"

"Aye," said Duncan grimly. "She's the one."

"And wouldn't I like to give her a piece of my mind," said Margaret, handing over the card. "'Tis a terrible thing to do to an innocent man."

Not all that innocent, Duncan thought, but Margaret's unwavering loyalty touched him. There had been little enough of that in his lifetime.

"The nerve of her, leaving you alone at the scene of a plane crash. Has she no heart?" Margaret declaimed. There was something of the actress in the elderly Scotswoman. "Has she no compassion?"

Duncan managed to ease his way from the gallery before Margaret saw to it that he was returned to the throne as ruler of Scotland.

Minutes later he was behind the wheel of his Land Rover with the small card propped on the dash.

He had Samantha's name, her company's name, her address, phone number, fax number and e-mail address.

He wondered if she was the one who had his heart.

Houston, July 4

THE DRESSMAKER knelt in front of Sam and frowned. "Darlin', I don't know what's wrong," the woman said through a mouthful of pins. "This gown fit you two weeks ago and now you're bustin' out all over."

Sam looked at her reflection in the long mirror and winced. The dressmaker was being kind. Even her cleavage had cleavage. She felt like a refugee from *Baywatch*.

Her sister Martie, already coiffed and dressed in her wedding gown, leaned close to Sam and lowered her voice. "Did you get a boob job, Sammy?"

Sam's cheeks flamed with embarrassment. "Of course not!" She tried to laugh, but no sound came out. "I—I bought one of those push-up bras. I guess it does a better job than I thought."

"Well, take it off right now," Martie ordered. "You can't walk down the aisle looking like that."

"What's wrong with the way I look?" Sam demanded. "I'm...busty." A statement she never thought she'd make in her lifetime.

"Busty?" Martie's voice rose sharply. "Honey, you're beyond busty. I don't know what on earth is going on, but this is my wedding day and—"

"Martie, listen to me." She grabbed her sister's hands in hers. "I'm having a problem with PMS. I'm as bloated as a sea sponge. You know I would do anything on earth for you, especially today, but there is nothing I can do about my breasts."

"I know, I know," Martie said. "It's just—well,

honey, I have to tell you the truth. With that low-cut gown you look like an exotic dancer.''

The idea was so ludicrous that they both started to laugh. ''You can rest assured I won't bump and grind my way down the aisle,'' Sam promised.

The dressmaker, who had been silent during this exchange, spoke up. ''I have an idea. It might not work but it's worth considering. Why don't I cut a length of cloth from the skirt and make a little insert for the bodice?''

''Anything,'' Sam said, desperate to divert attention from the size of her breasts. ''Cover me with a pink sheet. I don't care what you do.''

''No need to get testy,'' Martie said. ''I certainly never suggested anyone cover you up with a sheet.''

''I know you didn't,'' Sam said, instantly contrite. ''PMS, remember?''

''Maybe you should go see Dr. Bernstein. There might be something he could give you.''

The conversation was going from bad to worse. ''Great idea,'' Sam said. ''I'll make an appointment.''

Thank God the photographer chose that moment to make an appearance.

''Time for those candid shots we've been practicing,'' he said with a booming laugh. ''We want the bride over there. That's right, darlin', right by the window. No mother, right? How about the aunts, then? Where are they?'' His gaze landed on Sam. ''Va-voom! We better have fireproof film for you, sweet thang.''

It's your sister's wedding day, Sam told herself. She could blow up at that horse's butt of a photographer after the reception, when Martie and Trask were on their way to the airport. Just because she looked as if she had two beige beach balls stuffed under her dress was no reason for him to be sexist and rude. So she'd put on a little weight. Was it her fault she'd gained it all in her breasts?

The photographer snapped shot after shot of Martie posed by the enormous Palladian window while the dressmaker worked a miracle with the bodice of Sam's maid-of-honor gown.

"Last time I saw anything like this, I was four months gone," the woman said with a merry laugh. "I swear to you, I could see my breasts getting bigger by the second."

A wave of dizziness swept over Sam, and it took all of her strength to pretend it wasn't happening. "I have PMS," she stated loudly for all to hear. "That's all. *PMS.*"

"Oh, I wasn't implyin' you were preggers, darlin', just—"

"Pregnant?" Martie's voice carried clear from the other side of the room. "Who's pregnant?"

"Nobody," Sam shot back. *"Nobody!"*

An uncomfortable silence fell over the room, and it occurred to Sam that she might have sounded a tad harsh, but it needed to be said. All of this talk about her pneumatic breasts was making her very uncomfortable.

It wasn't as if she hadn't considered the possibility that she might be pregnant, because she had. She was an intelligent woman with a logical mind and she knew about cause and effect. She'd taken an enormous health risk, but thank God she was on the Pill.

She absolutely, positively could not be pregnant.

Normal stress could turn a woman's cycle upside down. Imagine what a plane crash could do. This was probably nothing but some kind of delayed reaction to everything that had happened.

Get real, Sam. Admit it. All roads lead straight to Duncan Stewart.

Sometimes, late at night, she found herself reliving that interlude in his arms. She could feel the strong, warm pressure of his mouth against hers, the way his powerful body responded to her touch, how she'd actually believed—if only for a moment—that she'd found her mate.

What a fool she'd been. Gullible, vulnerable, everything she'd sworn she never would be. Yet, despite everything, her anger battled with a desire so fierce and primal it challenged every belief about herself she'd ever held. How could she possibly want him after what he'd done? He was a manipulative lowlife who'd withheld his identity in order to pry information from her, and she'd played right into his hands, telling him all of her hopes and dreams for Wilde & Daughters Ltd.

He didn't plan that plane crash, Sam...or what happened afterward. That was fate, pure and simple.

Their lovemaking had had nothing to do with Sam Wilde and Duncan Stewart. Their lovemaking had been between a man and a woman who had faced death together and triumphed. A celebration of life.

Her hand rested briefly against her belly and she shivered.

Not possible, she told herself. *Not in a million years.*

Last week she'd picked up a home pregnancy test

at the supermarket, but the second she got it home, she realized how foolish she was being. But she hadn't returned it—or even tucked it away in the hall closet. It was still sitting on the dressing table in her downstairs powder room. And she was still ignoring it.

"Sam." Martie placed a hand on Sam's forearm. "The photographer wants you to pose with me."

Sam snapped back to the moment. Martie's beautiful face looked pinched and worried, and Sam was instantly contrite. The last thing Sam wanted to do was cast a shadow on the proceedings. The road to this day had been long and rocky enough for Martie and Trask.

She summoned up her widest, most photogenic smile. "I'm yours to command," she said brightly. "This is your day."

Sam stood and smoothed the skirt of the sleek oyster pink gown. Martie linked her arm through Sam's.

"Thank you," Martie said.

"For what?"

"For not giving me the lecture."

"Lecture?" She was starting to feel like a parrot. "What lecture?"

"The one about Daddy and his marry-or-else ultimatum."

"I came down pretty hard on you when you were engaged to Jason, didn't I?"

"Yes, you did," Martie said. "And you were one hundred percent right. I never loved him. The only reason I said I'd marry him was to keep my place in the family."

"I know," Sam said, remembering. "I wanted to

shake some sense into you, but you were so afraid of losing Daddy's love that you would have married a total stranger in order to hang on to it.''

"Remember the night of my engagement party?" Martie asked. "Jason's mother was complaining about everything from the hors d'oeuvres to the air-conditioning. I escaped to the ladies' room and there you were, smoking a cigarette and reading *Money* magazine.''

Sam hadn't thought about that night in ages, but her sister's words brought it all back. "I gave you quite an earful, didn't I?''

"All of it deserved," Martie said, "but there's one thing, especially, that I'll never forget. *If you don't love him, don't marry him.*''

A big fat lump lodged itself in the center of Sam's throat. "And you love Trask?''

"So much," Martie whispered. "Oh, Sammy! I pray you'll find someone to love the way I love him.'' She threw her arms around Sam and hugged her tight, then reared back and shot a wide-eyed look at Sam's prodigious bosoms. "Wow," she said, shaking her head. "I've got to get me one of those bras.''

Thirty miles northwest of Houston Intercontinental Airport

THE LIGHTS of the city twinkled in the distance, and for the first time since he left Glasgow twenty-four hours ago, Duncan wondered if he'd made a mistake.

He and Samantha Wilde were strangers to each other. Not even their lovemaking had changed that. He wasn't sure they could ever be more to each other than they had been on that April afternoon by Loch Glenraven. He wasn't even sure he wanted them to be. All he knew was that he had to see her again. Hear her voice. Smell the sweet scent of her skin.

If he didn't, he'd spend the rest of his life wondering if he'd let his last chance for happiness slip away without a fight.

"LOOK AT THEM," breathed Estelle Ross, Lucky's devoted assistant, as Martie and Trask took to the dance floor a few hours later. "Did you ever see a more beautiful couple in your life?"

"Never," said Sam, dabbing at her eyes with a lacy handkerchief designed for exactly that purpose. What was it about weddings that turned sane women into water fountains? "They look so happy, don't they?"

"Sublimely happy," Estelle agreed. "They're a match made in heaven."

Sam didn't believe in heaven-made matches for herself, but she was happy to make an exception for her sister.

"Are you gals blubbering again?" Lucky's booming voice sounded behind them. "Won't catch me cryin' on a happy day like this."

Sam and Estelle looked at each other and burst into laughter. Lucky had done his own share of crying during the wedding ceremony and, even now, his blue eyes looked suspiciously damp as he watched his middle child dance with her new husband.

"Your dance with Martie is coming up, Lucky," Estelle reminded him. "Do us proud." She smoothed the lapels of his dinner jacket with a familiar, affectionate gesture that tugged at Sam's heart.

Sam felt like giving her father a swift kick in the shins. What on earth was wrong with him, anyway? Couldn't he see that Estelle was head-over-heels in love with him and had been for as long as Sam could remember? People were so blind when it came to matters of the heart, and time was so—

She caught herself. Since when was she so sentimental? Her sisters were the sentimental ones in the family, not Sam. Sam relied on her assistant, Jack, to see to it that birthday cards went out when they should and important anniversaries were acknowledged.

Frankie hadn't been able to make it home for the wedding, but she'd sent a handmade quilt, embroidered with the newlyweds' names and the wedding date, and a charming videotape of herself reciting a poem for the happy couple. Sam, on the other hand, had presented them with a check tucked inside an oversize Hallmark card. She consoled herself with the fact that she'd hand-selected the card.

"Ms. Wilde?" One of the hotel's catering executives appeared at her side. "There's a gentleman outside who'd like to see you. I don't believe he's one of the invited guests."

"Did he give a name?" she asked as a funny light-headed feeling swept over her. It couldn't be. It simply wasn't possible.

The woman shook her head. "Afraid not, but he did tell me to give you this." She handed Sam a sprig of heather.

Sam's life seemed to pass before her eyes, with special attention paid to that afternoon beside the banks of Loch Glenraven.

"Ms. Wilde? Are you all right?"

"No." The word popped out before Sam had a chance to think. "I mean, yes. I'm fine." She stared at the sprig of heather clutched in her hand. This couldn't be happening. He was supposed to be on the other side of the Atlantic Ocean, in Scotland, for heaven's sake. He had absolutely no business being right here in Houston, on her turf. "Why don't you tell the gentleman that he can contact me Monday morning at the office."

The woman smiled coyly. "He told me you'd say that."

"He did, did he?" Sam felt her hackles rise. She liked to think she was dependable but not predictable. "Then you can tell him he was right."

"I really think you'd better come out to the lobby and speak with him, Ms. Wilde."

Sam placed a hand on the woman's forearm and lowered her voice. "This is my sister's wedding reception," she said in icily formal tones. "These people are my family and friends. If the anonymous gentleman wishes to speak with me, he can call my office on Monday."

"Ms. Wilde," the woman said, beads of sweat forming at her temples, "I *urge* you to see the gentleman. He said—" She hesitated, an angry red flush rising up her throat. "I just can't believe he means this, but he said if you don't talk to him— Well, he said he'd strip naked and wait for you in the lobby."

"He said *what?*"

"He said he'd strip naked, Ms. Wilde, and I'm telling you here and now that must *not* happen! We have a bar mitzvah going on in the west wing, lots of little children running around. If one of them—''

"You don't have to explain," Sam said. "I understand your predicament."

"Is there a chance he's joking?"

The woman looked so hopeful that Sam hated to dash her spirits.

"Oh, he'd do it," Sam said. "Have no doubt about that."

"Please, Ms. Wilde," the woman said, "I'm begging you. We can't have a naked man in the lobby."

Martie and Trask waltzed by. They looked like the couple on top of the wedding cake. Blissfully happy.

She couldn't let Duncan Stewart ruin their day. Not even if seeing him again might ruin hers.

"Sammy!" Estelle called after her. "Where are you going? They'll be cutting the cake any time."

"Two minutes, Estelle. I'll be back before they finish dancing."

She followed the hotel executive through the long carpeted hallway that led to the enormous formal lobby. Built in the eighties during the oil boom, the lobby was pure Texas, a hymn to marble and gilt and glorious all-American excess. She wondered how it must look to his Scottish eyes and then she berated herself for entertaining the thought.

Who cared how it looked to him? He wasn't going to be in town long enough for it to matter.

"He was here a second ago," the hotel executive said, glancing around the wide expanse of open space.

"Don't worry," Sam said. "You go about your business. I'll wait here for him."

"If you're sure—"

"I'm positive. This won't take long."

The woman didn't need any encouragement. She turned and fled to the safety of her office.

Sam considered following her. It would serve him right. Let him strip and do the Highland fling, for all she cared. He wasn't her responsibility. If they hauled him off to jail, buck naked and in handcuffs, she wouldn't lift a finger to help him.

Unfortunately, that was when she made her fatal mistake and turned to look at him.

He was standing to the left of the enormous front door, partially shielded by a mirrored column. He wasn't wearing a kilt, but he might as well have been. When she looked at him, she saw the rugged beauty of the Highlands, the mountains and the rivers, those crystalline lakes, the sense that all things were possible.

Which was exactly why she couldn't turn away from him now. If she was ever going to put that interlude behind her, she'd have to go face-to-face with the man she'd shared it with.

DUNCAN HEARD the sound of her high heels clicking against the marble floor before he saw her. A quick, staccato tattoo that sounded anything but welcoming.

"What the *hell* are you doing here?" she demanded.

He stepped out of the shadows to face her. His memory of her beauty fell far short of the reality. The face of an angel, the body of a temptress. All he could do was stare at her in awe.

"I'm waiting," she said, her voice cold as the marble all around them. "Did you come all this way to stare at me?"

Nothing had prepared him for the sight of her. His memory hadn't come close to doing her justice.

"You are magnificent, Samantha," he said by way of tribute. "A goddess."

He noted the blush that stained her cheeks. The goddess was human.

"Thank you," she said. "If that's all you came here to say, I'll return to my sister's wedding."

He reached for her hand but she snatched it out of his grasp.

"Don't even think about it," she warned, her cornflower blue eyes flashing a warning. "You have no right to touch me."

"Lassie, I—"

"My name is Samantha," she snapped. "What's yours?"

The barb was well-aimed and well-deserved. He would not deny that fact. "I won't go before I've said my piece, Samantha."

"There's nothing you can say that could possibly interest me." She said it as if she meant it.

"Not even that I'm here to collect my money?"

"Money?" She stared at him in obvious disbelief. "What money?"

"My ten thousand dollars." He paused for effect. "American."

She opened her mouth to say something then stopped. The red in her cheeks grew brighter. "I hope you're joking."

"I never joke."

"Well, you can't possibly be serious about this."

"The agreement was ten thousand dollars American for a flight to Loch Glenraven. We landed on her shores."

"Excuse me," she said, "we *crashed* on her shores."

"A difference in semantics, not location."

"We were almost killed."

"But we are still alive."

"I refuse to continue this ridiculous conversation."

"I'll take cash or a personal check."

"I wouldn't give you a plug nickel," she shot back. "Not if you were starving to death."

She wheeled and started to walk away, but he stepped in front of her.

"I should have told you who I am, lassie. I would not hurt you for the world."

"You're still not getting the money."

"You judge me too harshly."

"I don't judge you harshly enough. If you had any consideration whatsoever for my feelings, you wouldn't be here on my sister's wedding day."

"I did not know this was your sister's wedding day."

"Well, someone must have told you something, Mr. Stewart. How else could you find me?" Her words were measured, but he noted that her face had drained of color.

"One of your neighbors told me where I could find you," he said, feeling the edges of his quick temper begin to fray. "The particulars were of little interest to me."

"And there's one of many differences between us," she said. She passed a hand across her forehead.

"These particulars are of great interest to me. Now, if you'll excuse me—"

She turned once again, took two steps away from him, then stopped.

"Lass?" He moved toward her. "Is something wrong?"

"N-nothing. I'm just a little light-headed." She lowered her head, and he saw the quick rise and fall of her breasts. Strange, he hadn't remembered her breasts as being quite so round or full.

He rested his hand on her right shoulder. "You need to sit down."

"I'm fine," she said, but she didn't sound that way at all to him. Her voice was shaky and thin, and a sheen of perspiration glazed her forehead.

"Lean on me. I'll find you someplace to sit."

"I don't want to sit." She swayed gently and he gripped her other shoulder, as well. "They're going to cut the cake. I have to—"

She stopped abruptly, a puzzled expression on her face, then fainted dead away.

Chapter Five

"Samantha." His voice floated in her left ear and drifted out through her right. "Can you hear me?"

Of course she could hear him. But that didn't mean she intended to let him know that.

Maybe he'd go away if she refused to open her eyes.

She squeezed her eyes tightly shut and lay still, trying to picture her surroundings. He must have carried her into the ladies' room near the bank of elevators and placed her on the pale blue couch with the brocade pillows that she'd noticed on one of her earlier visits. She could smell the tiny bowls of lavender potpourri they kept on the dressing tables.

"Too much champagne," she heard him say. "It's felled more Highlanders than single malt."

Fat lot he knew. She hadn't taken so much as a sip of the bubbly.

"Open your eyes," he urged.

She ignored him. Sooner or later he'd realize he was in the women's bathroom and go find an actual woman to help her.

He stood up and took a few steps away from her.

She resisted the urge to peek, even when she heard the sound of rushing water, followed by returning footsteps.

"I do not want to scare you, lassie, but—"

She shrieked and sat straight up, heart thundering, as water sluiced down her cheeks.

"Are you *crazy?*" Her voice climbed into the dogs-only zone. "You threw water on me."

"I didn't throw it," he said. "I sprinkled."

"Have you lost your mind? You could have given me a heart attack."

"I was worried, lass. The next step was to find medical help."

"I don't need medical help." She motioned for him to hand her one of the powder blue guest towels stacked in the wicker basket. "All I did was faint."

"That's not a normal state."

"I haven't had a chance to eat since this morning. I'm hungry, that's all."

He looked skeptical, but she didn't particularly care.

"They don't serve food at American wedding parties?"

"I couldn't find anything I liked." She blotted her face and hair with the towel then folded it neatly and rested it on her lap. "You can go now," she said to him.

"That's not a good idea."

"It's a very good idea."

"You haven't accepted my apology."

Her stomach lurched alarmingly and she prayed she wouldn't have to make a run for one of the stalls.

"What difference does it make?" she countered. "The damage is already done."

"Damage?" He knelt in front of her so his eyes were on a level with hers. Those beautiful deep blue eyes.

Unfair, she thought, looking away. That was how this whole thing had started.

"What damage?" he asked.

"A figure of speech," she said. "Now will you please go? In case you've forgotten, this is a ladies' room."

He glanced around the room, making a production of peering under the doors to the stalls. "We're alone. I'm not bothering anyone."

"You're bothering me."

"I mean you no harm."

"I don't want to get into a debate with you, Mr. Stewart. It's not my fault if you have a guilty conscience."

"I should have told you who I was that afternoon, Samantha. I was wrong and I am sorry if my mistake in judgment hurt you in any way."

"Fine," she said. Tears burned behind her eyes. Mistake in judgment? That's how he thought of their lovemaking, as a mistake in judgment? She rose to her feet. "There's no point to any of this." *Don't talk to me. Don't look at me like that. Don't make me think any more than I have to.* "Ten thousand dollars is a small price to pay to get you out of my life."

"I am not a sentimental man," he said, "but what happened between us—"

"*What* happened between you?"

Both Sam and Duncan turned toward the door to

see Martie standing there like a fiery-haired angel in white lace.

Sam struggled to even out her jangled nerves before speaking.

"Don't tell me I missed the cake-cutting ceremony," she said, gliding toward her sister. She felt wobbly and vulnerable, and she prayed she wouldn't faint a second time.

"Everyone's waiting," Martie said, glancing pointedly from Sam to Duncan then back again. "Estelle said you were probably in the ladies' room." She looked again at Duncan. Question marks practically danced in her eyes.

"Then let's go!" Sam linked arms with Martie, ignoring Duncan as if he wasn't even there.

"Sammy," said Martie, "your hair's wet."

"It's a long story," Sam said, not looking at Duncan.

Martie disentangled herself from Sam and extended a hand toward the Scotsman. "Pardon my sister's bad manners," she said. "I'm Martie Wilde—" She grinned. "I mean, Martie Benedict. And you're—"

"Duncan Stewart."

There wasn't so much as a glimmer of recognition on Martie's face, a fact for which Sam was painfully grateful. The Scotsman's reputation had yet to cross the Atlantic, but it was only a matter of time.

"So," said Martie as they clasped hands, "how do you know my sister?"

"Martie," Sam interrupted before Duncan could speak. "Your new husband must be wondering where you are."

"We met in Scotland," Duncan said, ignoring Sam's agitation.

"Scotland?" Martie spun toward Sam. "When were you in Scotland?"

"You didn't know Samantha made a trip to Scotland?" Duncan asked, obviously surprised.

"Wait a minute," Martie said. "Was that the trip you made in April, just before my bridal shower?"

"Yes," Sam said. She wasn't about to offer any unnecessary information.

"You went to Scotland?" Martie asked again, as if she couldn't quite believe her own ears.

Sam nodded.

"Why?"

Sam swallowed hard. "Business."

"What business?"

"She was looking for me," Duncan offered helpfully.

Sam shot him a murderous look. "Why don't you just keep your mouth shut?"

"Sammy!" Martie looked horrified.

"Oh, stop staring at me like that, Martie," Sam snapped. "He deserved it."

Martie turned to Duncan. "So you met my sister in Scotland?"

"Aye," he said. "At an airport north of Glasgow."

"And?" Martie prodded.

"One more word," Sam said to Duncan, "and so help me, I'll—"

"I was her pilot," he said.

"And?" Martie prodded again.

"I flew her to her destination."

"That's it?" Martie looked terribly disappointed.

"And that's it."

"So if you were just her pilot, what are you doing here?"

"Coincidence," Sam broke in. "He, uh, he had to take a...he was supposed to fly a—"

"Businessman," Duncan offered.

"Yes," Sam went on, "he had to fly a businessman from Glasgow to Houston for—"

"For a conference," Duncan said. "Electromagnetic technology."

Martie considered them both for a long moment then sighed loudly. "You know, that's the funny thing about telling lies. Keep them simple, that's what I always say."

"What did it?" Duncan asked. "The electromagnetic technology?"

Martie nodded. "That was really a little much."

"Don't you have something to do?" Sam asked her. She was starting to feel desperate. "Like cut a wedding cake or toss a bouquet?"

"Oh, my God, I forgot!" Martie lifted her skirt above her ankles and flew to the door. "Join us, Duncan," she tossed over her shoulder. "Maybe I'll get to the bottom of this mystery before the honeymoon starts." She hurried toward the ballroom in a flurry of white lace.

"Over my dead body," Sam said to Duncan as soon as her sister was out of earshot. "Forget she said anything. I'm dis-inviting you."

"You can't do that. It's her wedding. She can invite whomever she pleases."

"You don't belong," she said bluntly. "You're a stranger."

"Not to you."

"*Especially* to me. What happened between us was an enormous mistake."

"'Twas no mistake."

"A mistake," she repeated. "Believe it or not, I don't make a habit of sleeping with strangers."

"Nor do I, Samantha. You have no worries on that account."

Fierce heat rose from the soles of her feet. "That, Mr. Stewart, is none of my business." It *was* her business, of course, but right now all she wanted was to get as far away from him as fast as she could.

"Still, it is something you deserve to know."

"A little late for that, wouldn't you say?"

"Aye," he said, "and for that I'm sorry. You deserved more consideration."

"I really don't want to have this conversation. We made a mistake. I don't see why it's necessary to talk about it."

"A mistake?"

"Of course. Now if you'll excuse me, I'm going to watch my sister and her husband cut their wedding cake, and you're not going to stop me."

IF SAM had expected Duncan Stewart to go quietly into that good night, she quickly found out how wrong she was. It seemed as if he was always within reach, those dark blue eyes of his fastened on her with laserlike precision. Was he serious about the ten thousand dollars? The idea seemed absurd to her, but then so did everything else that had happened since that ill-fated flight to Glenraven. Just because he was an artistic genius didn't mean he was rich. And she knew enough about castles and titles to know that they didn't necessarily translate into wealth. Maybe he needed the money to put toward a new Cessna to replace the one they'd wrecked along the shores of Loch Glenraven.

Still, she couldn't fault Duncan Stewart on his manners. He mingled easily with people, identifying himself only as a pilot when they asked. A few of Martie's artist friends instantly recognized his name, but the Scotsman shrugged and said his was a common name back home. He stuck fairly close to her side but not so close as to set too many tongues wagging.

Of course, just the fact that she was with a man was bound to attract a certain amount of attention, especially since it happened about as often as Halley's comet sightings.

"So who is he, darlin'?" Lucky asked as they shared a dance toward the end of the evening. "Is it time to plan another wedding?"

"You can put away your tux, Daddy." She tried to keep her voice light and breezy. "Unless Frankie has a fiancé or two up her sleeve, you won't be playing father of the bride again any time soon."

"Didn't know they grew 'em so big in Scotland."

"Spoken like a true Texan," she said with a nervous smile. "We don't have the market cornered on size."

Lucky gave her a curious look. "So how did you two meet?"

"I told you, he was my pilot."

"And he's here because—"

"I don't really know," she said, "and I'm afraid I

don't really care.'' She'd long since learned that, with her father, the best defense was a good offense.

"There's something you're not telling me."

"I'm telling you everything I know."

"Baby girl, you haven't told me everything you know since you were three years old." To Sam's amazement, his eyes filled with tears.

"Daddy?" She stopped dancing. "Are you okay?"

"Just feeling some regrets today, darlin'. Wishing I'd made a few different choices." They picked up the rhythm again.

"We all have regrets," she said carefully. Since Lucky's heart attack some months back, he'd been prone to bursts of high emotion, and for the first time, she was beginning to understand how that felt.

"Martie and Francesca—I made mistakes with them, too, but they found a way to forgive me."

"Forgive you? I don't understand."

"You were always so smart and seemed so happy that I didn't bother to look deeper, to find out what you really needed."

"Daddy, I—"

"No, don't interrupt me, darlin'. Let me get this off my chest. You needed something your sisters didn't."

"I really wish you—"

"You needed the kind of parents Julia and I didn't know how to be."

"You did your best for us. I know that."

"I wasn't around. This damn business—"

"The business is what kept a roof over our heads. I understand that."

"It was more than that, darlin'. Same thing that

busted up the marriage. Julia and I were too damn selfish to see what was right in front of us.''

She tried to make light of his statement because she knew no other way to deal with his revelations. ''You did your best.''

''The hell we did.'' His tone was fierce. ''We did what was best for us, not what was best for you.''

''I don't know what you want me to say.'' What he was saying was true, but she hadn't the stomach for hurting him with the admission.

His expression softened as he looked at her and she remembered suddenly how much she loved him, despite their problems. ''Nothin' you can say, darlin'. What's done is done, but lately you've got me worryin' that your mamma's and my mistakes are keepin' you from finding your own happiness.''

''I am happy.''

''You're alone, darlin'. You can't be happy. You're not gettin' any younger, Sammy. It's time you started thinking about the future.''

''I *have* been thinking about the future, Daddy. Wilde & Daughters is in trouble. If we don't—''

''Not tonight, darlin'. Haven't you heard a word I've been sayin'?''

''You said that last week and last month and the month before that. If it isn't the right time very soon, it'll be too late for all of us.''

''We're the best jewelers in this country, darlin'. Ain't nothin' goin' to change that.''

''We might be the best, Daddy, but we're no longer the most successful. Not when it comes to the bottom line. We're hemorrhaging profits faster than I can ap-

ply a tourniquet. We need help or we're going to find
ourselves gobbled up.''

"Darlin', we've had ourselves slow times before
and we'll have slow times again after I'm gone. You
get only one chance at this life and you'd make me
real happy if I knew you understood that as well as
you understand the bottom line.''

There was no use talking to him when he was like
this. Her father operated on a different plane, one that
had nothing to do with reality. He'd always been a
seat-of-his-pants kind of businessman, but since his
heart attack, his approach to business had become
even more idiosyncratic.

"I want you to be happy," he was saying again.
"A husband, a family...is that too much to ask?''

"You never managed to make it work, Daddy,"
she pointed out. "We Wildes don't seem to be too
good at happy endings. Why should I be any different?'' Her mother had just ended another marriage.
Lucky had chalked up quite a few of them. Obviously, the gene that defined marital success had
passed them by. "Fortunately, marriage doesn't interest me. It never has and it never will.''

"I'm an optimist, darlin'.'' He gestured toward
Martie and Trask who were dancing together, bathed
in a golden glow of happiness. "Miracles happen.
One day you'll come to me out of the blue and say
you've found the right man and that'll be the happiest
day of my life.''

She forced a laugh. "I don't think you're in danger
of hearing that any time soon.''

"Can't blame an old man for hoping.''

She patted his arm. "You worry too much," she

said lightly. "What you need is a good fishing holiday."

"Funny you should mention that, darlin'. Dr. Bob and I are heading north first thing in the morning."

Sam thanked her lucky stars as her father launched into one of his favorite fishing stories. All things considered, she'd rather talk about trout than marriage any day of the week.

"WHO IS SAMANTHA dancing with?" Duncan asked the woman standing beside him at the bar.

The small red-haired matron squinted in the direction of the dance floor. "That's Lucky," she said, then looked at Duncan. "You don't know the father of the bride?"

"No," said Duncan, "but I think it's time I rectified that."

He put down his glass of champagne then strode across the dance floor toward Sam and her father. He stopped next to them.

"Good evening," he said, nodding in Lucky's direction.

Samantha glared daggers at him but he chose not to notice.

"We were talking about you," her father said. He stopped dancing with Sam and extended his right hand to Duncan. "I'm Lucky Wilde."

"Duncan Stewart."

The older man's grip was strong and sure. "Glad you could join us," he said cordially. "Sammy says you're a pilot."

"I am." This time he would tell the entire truth. "I'm also an artist."

Samantha stepped between the two men. "If you'll excuse us, Mr. Stewart, my father owes me a waltz."

Lucky looked at his daughter and chuckled. "She doesn't want to dance, Duncan, she wants to talk business."

"Daddy, that's really not any of his concern."

"Can you believe it?" Lucky continued. "Her own sister's wedding and my gal can't keep her mind off business. You dance with her, young man. Maybe you can show her how to have fun."

Samantha's eyes glittered with tears as she moved into Duncan's arms. "What is it you want from me?" she whispered, ducking her head against his shoulder. She spoke so softly he could barely make out her words. "I already told you I'd pay the ten thousand dollars."

"I don't want your money, Samantha."

"Then what *do* you want?" The catch in her voice made him feel like a bastard.

"I don't know that, either," he said, "just that I needed to see you again."

His words took Sam's breath away. She pressed her forehead against his shoulder and let the tears fall onto the fabric of his jacket.

"Why didn't you stay in Scotland where you belong?" she managed finally. "I would have forgotten you eventually."

"Maybe that's why I didn't."

"What happened between us wasn't real," she said. "You must know that."

"Aye," he said. "That's what I've told myself a

thousand times since that day but I can't seem to make myself believe it."

"You should believe it," she said, "because it's true. That woman wasn't me. I'm not passionate or spontaneous or any of those things you thought I was. I don't have a romantic bone in my body."

"You don't know yourself as well as you think, lassie. The woman I made love to was all those things and more."

"You're wrong," she said, pulling away from him the second the music stopped. "You're seeing what you want to see and not what's really there." She smoothed her hair with a nervous gesture. "I don't know why I'm talking about this at all with you." Or why she felt as if she was wearing her heart embroidered on her sleeve.

"Everybody!" Estelle's voice rang out over the din. "All you single gents come on over to the bandstand. It's garter time!"

Duncan refused to move from Sam's side until Estelle, a strong-minded woman, threatened to make a scene if he didn't join in the fun.

"You get your fanny over there, honey," Estelle said to him with a broad wink. "Catch the garter and you'll be the next one to tie the knot."

Reluctantly Duncan joined the group of men on the dance floor while the groom led his bride to a chair at the edge of the bandstand.

His only experience with American bridal rituals was what he'd seen in Hollywood movies, so he felt the odd man out.

The bride coyly lifted the hem of her gown to expose her ankles and calves. The groom ran his hand

over her instep, her ankle, then higher, higher, higher,
until he looped his thumb around a frilly blue satin
garter just above her knee. The men around him
cheered lustily as the groom slid the garter from his
bride's leg then waved it overhead like a trophy in
some medieval festival.

Then, before Duncan knew what was happening,
the groom flung the garter into the crowd of men. A
raucous cry went up as grown men grabbed for the
scrap of satin and elastic that spun past them and
landed on Duncan's head.

The band launched into a funeral dirge while the
good-natured Texans clapped Duncan on the back and
made jokes about him being the next to walk the
plank. What plank? he thought. And why a garter?

As for Sam, she watched the proceedings with apprehension. It was all too neat, too pat, as if unseen
hands were conspiring to tie their fates together,
whether they wanted them tied together or not. She
knew Martie would see to it that she caught the bouquet if she had to hand-deliver it right into Sam's
outstretched hands. The thing to do was leave. Just
slip out the door behind the bar and make a run for
freedom. She turned and was about to make a break
for it when Martie called out, "Where are you going,
Sammy? It's time to toss the bouquet."

Short of feigning her own death, there was no way
out. She wouldn't hurt Martie for the world, not on
her wedding day. Sam lined up with the other single
women as Martie glided to the top of the staircase
and stopped right beneath the crystal chandelier so
the photographer could snap another dozen pictures.
Sam barely recognized her sister. The Martie she'd

known was an eccentric artist who rarely did anything conventional. But there she was, in her lacy white wedding gown, tossing her bridal bouquet like millions of other brides before her.

It must be love, Sam thought in bewilderment. Nothing else could explain the change in Martie.

"Okay, ladies," the new bride called out. "Get ready!" She winked broadly at Sam, who devoutly wished she could disappear. Sixty pairs of eager arms raised heavenward in anticipation. Sam clasped her hands behind her back. If Martie threw the bouquet in her direction, she'd duck.

The emcee tapped the microphone. "Drumroll, please. On the count of one...two...*three!*"

The bouquet tumbled through the air, ribbons streaming, and headed straight for Sam. Sam ducked. The bouquet lost altitude. Sam moved to the right. Perfect. It would whiz right on by her.

Or it would have if one of the dopey bridesmaids hadn't made a grab for it and somehow changed its trajectory, putting it on a collision course with Sam's nose. She raised her hands to protect herself and caught the flowers instead.

Sam looked across the room at Duncan, who was still clutching that foolish blue garter. She held up the flowers. He twirled the garter around his index finger. They looked like two prisoners trying to escape from Alcatraz.

Years ago her cousin Bobby and a woman named Phyllis had caught the garter and the bouquet at Aunt Lula's wedding. They'd thought it meant they had to get married to each other and so they eloped to Mexico that very night. The hangover had lasted longer than the marriage. Thank God neither Sam nor Duncan were that dumb.

The laughing horde of single women swarmed all over Sam and pushed her toward the center of the dance floor where a lone wooden chair waited for her. Duncan was being swept her way on a sea of bachelors. She noticed that he looked quite bewildered by this turn of events—and she also noticed that his bewilderment was quite appealing.

"You should have left when you had the chance," she said to him as she sat on the chair. "You're a foreigner. You shouldn't have to see this embarrassing American ritual."

"Don't pay her any mind," said Jo Marie Albright, Wilde & Daughters' best saleswoman. "Nothing wrong with this ritual." She winked broadly. "Not if you're lookin' for someone to love."

"I'm not looking for anyone to love," Sam proclaimed in a loud, clear voice.

"Everyone knows that about you, Sammy," Jo Marie said, shaking her head. "But I still like to think miracles happen."

"Looks like you're out of luck," Ted Di Mentri said, elbowing Duncan in the ribs. Ted was one of Martie's old high school pals. "She's not buyin' what you're sellin'."

Duncan didn't say anything, but the deer-in-the-headlights expression on his face spoke volumes.

"I refuse to feel sorry for you," Sam said as they urged her to lift her skirt to the knee. "You're only slightly embarrassed. I, however, am totally humiliated."

"Oh, be quiet, Sam," Martie called out, "and let the man do his job."

Duncan's dark brows drew together in a scowl. "And what would that job be?"

Ted's grin was wolfish. "You get to slide that little honey of a garter up this pretty gal's leg."

"C'mere, darlin'," Sam said, playing for the crowd. "I want to give you a little incentive."

Duncan leaned forward. She looped her arms around his neck and pressed her lips to his ear.

"Just *do* it," she hissed, "and I'll give you the ten thousand dollars."

If this whole miserable experience went on any longer, she would leap headlong into the remains of the wedding cake.

Duncan felt like a fool as he knelt in front of her, dangling the blue garter from his right index finger. Music swelled, the kind of music he'd heard in strip joints and cheap pubs.

"Go for it!" someone yelled. A burst of wild applause crashed over him.

She extended her right foot. He encircled her ankle with his left hand and her eyes widened. Beneath the sharp-tongued anger was a vulnerable—and very beautiful—woman. She sat stiffly on the wooden chair, her posture ramrod straight, as if she were waiting for the firing squad to aim their rifles. She didn't belong there any more than he did. He wasn't sure how he knew that, only that it was a fact.

I'm not going to hurt you, lassie.

He slid the garter over her foot, her arch, her ankle, then snaked it slowly up the curved muscle of her calf. Her legs were long and slim and beautifully shaped. A work of art made flesh and blood. He remembered how those legs had felt, wrapped around his hips, as he—

"Duncan!" she exclaimed.

He realized his hand was skating over her knee and up her thigh. "Bloody hell!" he muttered then pulled away as she let her skirt drop.

The din around them was deafening. He felt foolish, surrounded by these laughing, happy Americans who had no idea who he was or what he was about. He wondered if they knew anything at all about Samantha, the woman who'd grown up in their midst.

"This is your dance," the emcee called out. "Everyone, let's hear it for next year's happy couple—" He paused, aiming a pointed look in their direction. "Your names?"

"Sam," Sam mumbled.

"Harvey," Duncan said.

"Harvey?" Sam started to laugh.

"Nobody noticed, lassie," he said as he took her in his arms. "Nobody cares."

They took a few tentative twirls around the floor and then everyone else joined them. He couldn't draw a breath without bumping into another dancer.

"I thought I—" Samantha stopped and he felt her sway against him. "The heat," she murmured. "Too crowded…"

He danced her quickly across the room, past the curious glances and stage whispers, and out onto the terrace.

"You have to stop doing this," she said as she breathed deeply of the cool night air. "That's twice tonight you've saved me from making a fool of myself.''

"Do you feel better now?"

"Absolutely." She smiled at him. "Thank you."

He turned and started toward the stairs.

"Duncan!" She grabbed the hem of his jacket. "Where are you going?"

"Go back to your family, lassie. You were right. I don't belong here."

"Wait!" *What's your problem, Sam? Isn't this what you wanted? In another minute he'll be out of your life for good.* "I mean, how will you get back to your hotel? Did you rent a car or—"

"I'll call for a taxi."

"Where are you staying? I'd be happy to—"

"I'm going home, Samantha. To Glenraven."

She felt as if the air had been knocked out of her. "At least let me drive you to the airport. It will take forever to get a cab way out here on a Sunday night. Besides, you probably don't have any idea when the next plane leaves. You might be stuck at the airport for hours and hours. I can't let you do that." *Why can't you let him do that, Sam? What possible difference can it make to you?*

His survival instinct, honed to a fine point since his divorce, told him to ignore the gleam of tears in her cornflower blue eyes, warned him to leave while he still could. He was a sophisticated man of thirty-seven years. They both knew he would have no trouble making his way to the airport.

It was time he left.

She fainted into your arms twice tonight. Will you leave her here to drive home alone?

He wasn't her husband or her guardian. Where she went and how she managed to get there were no business of his.

But he remembered the way she'd felt in his arms when she passed out. The languid grace. The extreme vulnerability. Where were her family and friends? Didn't anyone know she needed help?

"You're right," he said, against his better judgment. "Would you let me make some calls from your house?"

"Of course," she said. "And I'll write out your check while you're there."

Just so they both understood what was important.

Chapter Six

Duncan insisted on doing the driving, which to Sam's way of thinking was one of the more ridiculous things she'd heard all night.

"That's absurd," she said. "You don't know the first thing about Houston. It will take us two hours to go twenty miles."

"I'm a quick study."

"I don't doubt it," she said. Then a thought occurred to her. "I'm an excellent driver, in case that's what's worrying you." For all she knew, the American prejudice against women drivers might be a Scottish pastime, as well.

"I don't doubt that you are."

"You think I'm going to faint again, don't you?"

"The thought had occurred to me."

"I got along just fine for thirty-two years before you showed up, Duncan Stewart. I'm sure I can manage to get myself home in one piece."

"I'm driving," he said, taking the keys from her. "I won't argue the point any longer."

She wasn't sure if he sounded protective or hostile.

Either way, she didn't like it. He had no right to either emotion, not when it pertained to her.

She directed him out of the parking lot to the highway. "You'll get off at the third exit," she said, "then take the first right."

"Bloody hell," he muttered as he shifted into gear. "I canna get used to driving on the right."

"You'd better get used to it in the next five seconds or I'm jumping out of this car no matter what you say."

She directed him street by street toward her condo while he concentrated on his driving. Every time a car whizzed by in the opposite lane, he found himself flinching. Didn't they know they were on the wrong side of the road?

"You really should have let me drive," she said. "We'd be there by now."

"I'm enjoying myself," he lied.

"I'm not," she said. "Your driving stinks. Pull over and let me get behind the wheel."

Her request only made him more determined to see it through. He was a proud Scotsman, and that meant seeing a job to completion. Forty minutes later, they pulled up in front of her two-story town house.

She was out of the car in a flash and on her way up the curved walkway by the time he turned off the ignition. He joined her at the front door.

"I have a security system," she warned him. "Once I put my key in the lock, we have thirty seconds to get inside so I can deactivate the alarm."

"This is a dangerous place?"

"Every place is dangerous," she said. "Don't you know that?"

He hated the thought of her barricaded behind alarms and wires and high fences. There was no need for that where he came from. He told himself that it was not his business, that this was her life and she was free to live it any way she chose. Still, he found himself shielding her body from view as she inserted the key into the lock.

Sam wondered why he was standing so close to her. "Could you move a little?" she asked politely. "You're blocking out the light." She also wondered why, all things considered, she wasn't more annoyed with him.

She turned the key.

Thirty, twenty-nine, twenty-eight...

She stepped inside.

Twenty-seven, twenty-six, twenty-five...

So did Duncan.

Twenty-four, twenty-three, twenty-two...

He stood so close to her that she was practically in his arms. She'd have to take him to task about that when she had a moment.

Twenty-one, twenty, nineteen...

She had to deactivate the alarm before the entire Houston police department showed up on her doorstep.

Eighteen, seventeen, sixteen, fifteen...

"There!" She finished pressing in the code and waited for the green light to flash in recognition. "See? It wasn't so terrible. We weren't captured by terrorists. You can give me a little breathing room now."

He didn't seem inclined to do it, so she stepped

around him and dropped her beaded purse on the Parsons table in the foyer.

"The telephone is in the kitchen," she said. "The directory is on the bookshelf near the desk in the corner. I'll be right back."

Duncan watched her disappear up the staircase in a swirl of pink satin and lace. Beautiful and unreachable. He knew the combination well. He also knew to avoid it at all costs. Why was he going along with this charade about the ten thousand dollars? He didn't want or need her money. If he had the brains he was born with, he would be long gone by the time she came downstairs.

He saw a formal room to the right of the stairs and a dining room to the left. He followed the narrow hallway to the back of the apartment where it opened up into a large, high-ceilinged kitchen with paddle fans and every modern convenience he could imagine and a few he couldn't. The directory was where she said it would be, and he flipped quickly to the section marked Taxicab Service and chose a number.

"I need a ride to the airport," he said. "As soon as you can get here."

"We'll need your address."

He swore, then hung up the phone. He didn't know the address. He wasn't even sure he was still in Houston proper, for that matter. He was trapped until she returned and gave him the street number.

SAM CONSIDERED the wisdom of locking herself in her bedroom and waiting for him to leave, but decided that was the coward's way out. Not that she had anything against being a coward. It was just that the man was so stubborn, he might take a week or two before he took the hint.

No, the best way to go about this was to be forthright and honest. And if that failed, lie through her teeth.

She pulled on a pair of jeans and shrugged into a navy blue sweatshirt with frayed sleeves. Quickly she pulled the pins from her elaborate hairdo then dragged her fingers through the mass of waves. Barefoot, she hurried downstairs to see him on his way.

She fished her checkbook out of her desk drawer then marched into the kitchen. "I'll write you a check and then—" She stopped when she realized she was the only one in the room. Had she been upstairs long enough for him to call a cab and leave? He wouldn't do that. Still, he had to be somewhere. She stepped into the hallway and noticed light seeping from under the closed door of the powder room. Mystery solved.

She decided to make some coffee to fortify him for his trip. A terrible thought occurred to her as she pulled the pot from the cupboard. What had she done with the pregnancy test she'd bought? The last time she'd noticed it, it was on the vanity in the powder room. The same powder room where Duncan Stewart was right that minute.

A sense of dread filled her but she tried to push it away with a dose of common sense. She wasn't the kind of woman who left things lying around like that. She was orderly and precise to a fault. No, she must have put it away in the upstairs linen closet, the one with all the other things she'd never use.

No cause for alarm, she told herself as she turned on the cold water to fill the pot. Unless he started rummaging around for extra towels or something, the odds of him stumbling over the home pregnancy kit were about a million to one.

She heard the bathroom door open, then the sound of male footsteps approaching. She had the awful feeling that the odds had just lowered dramatically.

"What is this?" He sounded more like a Scots warrior than ever, and her hands began to shake.

Sam kept her back to him while she filled the pot. "What's what?" she asked in what she hoped was a casual tone of voice.

"Don't play games, Samantha."

"I'm not play—" She stopped midword. Who was she kidding? She knew exactly what he meant. She put down the glass pot then turned.

He stood in the doorway to the kitchen. The pink-and-blue box looked very tiny in his enormous hand.

"It's a home pregnancy kit," she said, drawing her hands down the sides of her jeans. "But you already knew that."

"Is it yours?"

She nodded. "It's mine." She hadn't watched *Court TV* for nothing. She knew how this worked. Answer only the question posed. If he wanted more information out of her, he was going to have to pry.

"And?" He took a step closer.

She would have taken a step backward but that would mean climbing into the kitchen sink. "And nothing," she said.

"Are you pregnant?"

"Take another look at the box, Sherlock." Her temper was stretched to the breaking point. "It's un-opened."

"Do you think you're pregnant?"

Her eyes burned with angry tears. "I think that's none of your business."

"I think you're lying."

"I don't particularly care what you think."

"Your breasts are bigger," he said, assessing her with his eyes. "Your face is fuller."

She grabbed the bag of chocolate chip cookies on the counter. "Want one?" she asked, ripping open the bag and stuffing a cookie in her mouth. "Terrible for the waistline, but what a way to go."

"What is this about?"

"Nothing," she said. "Certainly nothing that has anything to do with you."

"You've slept with someone else since we made love?"

An ugly flush moved up her throat to her face. She maintained her silence. No matter what she said, she was doomed.

"Answer me," he said in a tone that would unnerve a lesser woman. "You owe me that much."

"I owe you ten thousand dollars for the plane ride," she said. "Answers will cost you a lot more."

"I'm not known for my patience."

"That makes two of us," Sam said. She brushed cookie crumbs from her hands. "Why don't I write you a check and you can run along."

She tried to maneuver past him, but he blocked the entrance.

"Weren't you supposed to call for a cab?" she asked.

"When were you planning to tell me about this?"

"Never," she snapped. "Is that what you want to

hear? I'd hoped I could live my entire life without having this conversation." Oh, God, her voice was beginning to tremble. She sounded like she was yodeling. "I thought I might have a problem, but I was wrong. Case closed."

"You didn't miss a period?"

He wasn't letting her slip past him, physically or emotionally.

"It was the crash," she said. "It disrupted my cycle."

"The crash was three months ago."

"So it's taking me a while to get back on track."

"There's more to it than that."

"No!" Her voice rose in agitation. "That's all it is." She refused to allow it to be anything else.

"You fainted, lassie." His tone softened and the look in his eyes made her legs go weak. "Your breasts are larger and your belly—"

Her hands instinctively cupped her belly and she lowered her head to hide her tears.

"I can't be pregnant," she whispered. "This isn't what I wanted."

"At last," he said. "Something we can agree on."

She wanted to smack him but didn't have the energy.

"Take the pregnancy test," he said.

"This is my problem." She snatched the box from him. "I'll take care of it myself."

"Don't push me away, Samantha," he warned. "I won't go before this is settled."

"I resent your tone of voice," she said, recovering her equilibrium. "This is my home, and if I tell you to leave, you're damn well going to leave."

He brushed away her words as if she hadn't said them at all. His eyes never left hers. "Could anyone else be the father?"

For a brief moment she considered lying to him but found she couldn't. "No," she whispered. "No one else."

"Then do it now."

The thought of knowing the truth was more than she could handle. "I can't do it now. You're supposed to run the test in the morning."

"That's not what it says on the box."

He was right. The words Use Any Time of Day were written across the front of the package in bold letters.

"All right," she said. "I'll do it and then we won't have to have this conversation again as long as we live."

She started toward the powder room with him right behind her.

"Don't even think it," she said from the bathroom doorway. "You're not coming in here with me."

"I want to watch when you run the test."

"Wait out there," she ordered. "This is a one-woman operation."

A few minutes later she returned with a specimen cup of urine.

"What happens next?" he asked.

She spread the instructions on the kitchen counter. "I put five drops of urine in that little well then wait three minutes."

"Only three minutes?"

"That's what it says." It hardly seemed long enough for something so momentous. "Either a plus sign or a minus sign will appear in this window.'' She met his eyes. ''And then we'll know.''

''Then get on with it, lassie.''

She carefully squeezed five drops into the well and set her timer. The instructions said it had to be exactly five drops or the test results could be badly skewed. She sat at the kitchen table. Duncan sat opposite her. Neither one said a word as the seconds ticked by silently.

Ding. Ding. Ding.

Her breath caught. She pushed back her chair and stood up. ''This is it,'' she announced. One of the least necessary observations she'd ever made.

''Aye,'' he said. ''This is it.''

She looked at the white plastic receptacle. A big red plus sign looked up at her. She closed her eyes then looked again. The big red plus sign was still there. She felt the way she had right after the plane crash, numb, elated, terrified, shell-shocked—all those things at the same time.

But mostly she felt scared.

''I'm pregnant,'' she said, as tears spilled down her cheeks. ''Oh, God.'' She leaned against the wall as the room seemed to spin around her. ''What am I going to do?''

Duncan met her eyes. ''There is only one thing you can do,'' he said. ''You're going to marry me.''

''That's not funny.''

''It wasn't meant to be.''

Her head felt as if it was filled with helium. Any second it would separate from her body and float off. She closed her eyes and pulled in a shaky breath. He was saying something, but she couldn't make out the words. Slowly she began to slide to the floor. Duncan caught her before she fell.

"Stop doing that," she murmured, letting her head drop onto his shoulder.

"Doing what, lassie?"

"Rescuing me. I don't need your help. Maybe I'd like falling down. You never give me the chance to find out."

"Aye," Duncan said as he carried her into the front room. "I can see that."

For the second time that night, he placed her on a sofa then went to the kitchen to fetch her a glass of water.

"Thank you," she said after taking a sip. "I don't know what's wrong—" She stopped, and a bitter laugh mingled with her tears. "Wait a minute, I *do* know what's wrong, don't I?" She buried her face in her hands and started to cry.

Duncan had never felt more useless in his life. She cried as if her heart was breaking, wrenching sobs that made his gut ache. He didn't know why he'd said what he had. A bad marriage was a prison unlike no other.

Bloody hell, he still hadn't quite comprehended the fact that she was pregnant with his child. Somewhere in his mix of confusion and anger, there was beginning in his marrow a fierce sense of elation. He remembered the last time and how it had ended. The one thing he knew, the only thing, was that this time would be different if he had to move heaven and earth to guarantee it.

"Stop staring at me," she snapped between sobs.

"Why don't you just call a cab and go back to Scotland where you belong?"

"I can't go now and leave you like this."

"Why not?" she demanded. "If you hadn't popped up here unexpectedly, you wouldn't even *know*."

"But I do know, and that makes all the difference."

She swatted at his arm with her left hand. "Can't you take a hint? I don't want you here, Duncan Stewart. I don't want you in my house."

"You shouldn't be alone right now."

"Why should now be any different?" Edgy laughter cut through her tears. "I've always been alone."

Oh, God, Sam thought. Where on earth had that come from? She'd read about wildly escalating estrogen levels that made pregnant women highly emotional, but she'd never read about the self-pity hormone kicking in. She'd never be able to look him in the face again.

Once again Duncan chose to court danger. He reached over and smoothed a lock of pale blond hair from her cheek. He felt her tears against his fingertips, the rose-petal softness of her skin.

"What's the matter with you?" she asked, her voice breaking. "Can't you take a hint? Go back to your castle where you belong."

He held her while she cried, smoothing her hair with his palm, saying things in the language of his grandmother and her grandmother before her. He wondered what had brought him to this place, what primitive understanding had coursed through his veins and told him to find her. The randomness of it all. The blind amazing luck.

Finally she stopped crying and pulled away from him. Her nose was red. Her eyes were puffy and swollen. Her hair needed combing. And it didn't matter a damn. Somehow she was still beautiful.

"Why did you come here?" she asked him.

He forced a smile. "To phone for a taxi."

She didn't smile back. "I mean, why did you come to Houston?"

"I don't know," he said honestly. How could he tell her about the Glasgow pub and the aching loneliness he'd felt every day since? "I had no choice in the matter."

She nodded as if it somehow made sense. "This surprised me as much as it surprised you."

"I doubt that."

"I was taking the Pill," she said. "You're not supposed to get pregnant on the Pill."

"But it happened."

Her hands cupped her belly, and he saw the look of bewildered wonder in her eyes. "Yes," she said quietly. "It did, didn't it?"

Another wave of bone-crushing fear gripped her, and she began to cry at the enormity of what had happened. She didn't know the first thing about babies. How could she possibly have one of her own?

And she didn't have a husband. She knew husbands were optional these days, but she couldn't help wanting to give her baby what she'd never known herself—two parents who not only loved her but lived with her on a daily basis. Not just when it was convenient or when work permitted or when the stars and the moon were in some kind of mystical alignment.

But all the time. Every day of the week. Every month of the year.

Crazy thoughts were popping into her mind at a dizzying rate. Her pregnancy would turn Wilde & Daughters Ltd. upside down. Martie would swoon with delight and turn Sam's life into one long baby shower. Estelle would fuss over her like a mother hen, making sure Sam took her vitamins and exercised and ate all the right foods. She probably wouldn't be able to draw in a single breath between now and her due date without someone staring over her shoulder and monitoring her oxygen intake.

And what about her staff and her clients and the inordinate amount of business travel she usually undertook between now and early autumn? How much of it could she do? More important, how much of it did she want to do?

The rumor mill was an amazing thing in the best of times. Sam's pregnancy would have it grinding out gossip at a record pace. They'd find out all about her and Duncan.

"Maybe the test was wrong," she said, grasping at straws. "That's why they package two tests in the one box. Just in case you think you made a mistake."

He looked skeptical, to say the least. "Ninety-eight percent accuracy rate," he said, reading the advertising copy on the box.

"So's the Pill," she said, "and see what happened."

He saw. "Then take the test again, lass, and see."

She did, and the results were the same. A bouncing-baby plus sign winked up at them.

"So now we know," she said, tossing the whole

mess into the garbage. "I'm definitely pregnant." And not just pregnant, but terrified and drowning beneath the weight of it all. And she heard herself saying all of that and more to him. The words spilled from her mouth, and there wasn't one damn thing she could do to stop the flood.

Duncan listened as she spoke, and much of what she said touched a similar chord in him. The lonely child who feigned independence until that independence became a barrier between herself and the rest of the world. He understood it. He knew how it felt to watch your parents bounce from mate to mate, dead certain that the next love would be the last one. How it felt to want what every other child took for granted.

"I want so much more for this baby," she said. "I wish—" She stopped and shook her head. "It doesn't matter what I wish. I'm pregnant and nothing can change that."

"Not every woman feels as you do," he pointed out.

"I know, but that's not my choice." She met his eyes. "Sorry, Duncan, but like it or not, you're going to be a father."

"I like it."

She felt a shot of adrenaline race through her veins. "You like it?"

"Very much." More than she could possibly imagine.

"We barely know each other. We're strangers."

"Marriage will change that."

"Now wait a minute." She stood up. "That's the second time you've said that tonight. You can't possibly mean it."

"'Tis the perfect solution, Samantha."

"Marrying a total stranger is the perfect solution? You've lost your mind."

He stood up, as well, reclaiming the height advantage. Obviously he also knew something about strategic positioning. "Think about it," he said. "We both know what it's like to have parents whose main concern is the pursuit of romantic happiness."

"The children take a back seat," Sam said. "But what does that have to do with our situation?"

"We can see to it that doesn't happen to our child, Samantha. A marriage based on a mutual goal rather than romantic love cannot fail."

"What mutual goal?" There was something wrong with his thesis, and she was determined to find it.

"A family a child can depend on."

Oh, God. How could she argue that? It was the one thing she'd prayed for as a little girl. "That sounds wonderful, but I don't see—"

"I want my child to know his father," he said bluntly. "The child will inherit Castle Glenraven one day and all that entails."

"And what if the child is a girl?" she asked.

"That makes no difference to me, lassie. My child will inherit. A legal marriage between us would guarantee it."

"Are you suggesting I marry you and move to Scotland?"

"Aye," he said.

"That's crazy," she said, not quite as forcefully as she might have liked. *Think about it, Sam. An entire ocean between you and six months of nosy questions and unsolicited advice.*

Her expression softened, and he moved closer. "We're not as backward as you might think, lass. We have fine doctors and modern hospitals, too."

"I never said you didn't." She paused as an idea—a crazy idea—began to take shape. "I see what you stand to gain by this marriage, but I'm not sure I see what I stand to gain."

He opened his mouth to speak, but she raised her hand to stop him.

"What we need," she said, "is some kind of agreement to spell out the terms."

He nodded. "I'm listening."

"The best arrangements are the ones that are beneficial to both parties." She was on a roll. Making deals was what she did for a living. She could almost feel her confidence returning. "Let me see if I understand your terms. You want a legal marriage and you want the child to be born in Scotland."

"Aye," he said, no longer certain where she was taking this.

"I see where that benefits you, but I don't see what it has to offer me."

"What is it you want?"

"You," she said, then realized how it sounded. "What I mean is, I want the same thing I wanted when I flew to Scotland to track you down. I want you to design for Wilde & Daughters."

"Lassie, I work on a grand scale. I can't imagine—"

"I know it will work," she interrupted. She mentioned one of his earliest pieces. "Imagine it in silver, maybe on a marble pedestal. A limited edition, numbered—it's a win-win proposition, Duncan. We get to be your exclusive dealer, and you get your name out there in front of millions of people who wouldn't have known a thing about you otherwise."

"And for that you'll marry me?"

Put up or shut up time, Sammy.

"Yes," she said, then said it again in a louder, stronger voice. "If we can agree to terms, I'll marry you."

Chapter Seven

It took all night. Duncan drank two pots of coffee while Samantha settled for milk. They argued the little points and negotiated the big ones and by the time the sun came up in the eastern sky, they had themselves a deal.

Sam looked at the stack of papers on the kitchen table. "You drive a hard bargain."

Duncan polished off the last of the coffee and pushed the cup away from him. "Aye, but no harder than you, lassie."

She'd approached it the way she approached any other business deal because that was exactly what it was. They were both practical, down-to-earth individuals who understood the terms of the agreement they'd hammered out. First and foremost, was the happiness of their child. Without that, they had nothing. This child would have two hands-on parents. There was no arguing that point for either one of them.

From there it had gotten interesting. Duncan refused to budge on the Scotland issue. Sam refused to

budge on signing him up with Wilde & Daughters
Ltd. under an exclusive contract.

"I'm giving up my country," she pointed out. "I
don't think what I'm asking of you comes close."

In the end he gave in. Oh, he muttered something
dark about crass commercialization, but she ignored
him. When the accolades started rolling in, he'd
change his tune soon enough.

And that left one final hurdle to be faced.

"When will you tell your family?" Duncan asked
as she fixed them each a bowl of cereal.

"How does our silver wedding anniversary
sound?" she asked, only half-kidding.

"You can't be serious, lassie."

"Lucky's off on a fishing trip," she said. "He'll
be out of touch for a few weeks." Martie and Trask
were on their honeymoon. Frankie was somewhere in
Hawaii. And her mother Julia could be just about anywhere on the globe.

"The thing to do is elope," she said. "They'll love
that."

And if she eloped, she wouldn't have to face the
inevitable round of questions. Elopements were synonymous with love. Any suspicions her father might
have about her hasty wedding would be allayed by
his basically romantic nature. Presented with a fait
accompli, there was nothing Lucky, or anyone else,
could do but wish them luck.

All in all, it was the only logical solution.

SAM MANAGED to grab her gynecologist's second appointment of the morning, and by ten-thirty she and
Duncan had confirmation of her pregnancy and of her

general good health. The office manager tried to set up a series of prenatal appointments, but Sam said she needed to consult her schedule before she could commit to specific dates. She could just imagine their surprise when she asked them to send her records to Scotland.

"With any luck, it'll be a Christmas baby," Duncan said as they left the office.

She met his eyes. "I know." A silly smile spread across her face. "Can you believe it?"

From there they went to meet with Sam's lawyer, who had Duncan's attorney on the speakerphone.

Unfortunately neither man agreed with the wisdom of Sam and Duncan's plan. Both men had endless reasons the marriage was destined for failure, but Sam and Duncan weren't listening. The baby was all that was important. If they could create a stable family life for their child, all of this endless bickering would have been worth it.

It took a few hours but at last a final draft of their prenuptial agreement was hammered out and presented to Sam and Duncan for their signatures.

Sam found herself strangely depressed as she looked at the pages of legalese that represented the rest of her life. She wasn't a romantic like her father. You wouldn't think the flat statement of terms would hit her so hard but it did. She took the pen from her attorney and signed her name in quadruplicate and tried very hard not to think of her sister Martie's radiant face as she took her wedding vows.

Duncan felt detached from the proceedings. His first wedding had been born of hopes and dreams. It had ended up in despair. Maybe this way was better.

Samantha saw their marriage as a business arrangement and nothing more. One look at her face, so cool and lovely and distant, and he knew he couldn't delude himself into believing she felt anything at all for him. The glorious woman he'd made love to had been replaced by a stranger. He had traveled from Scotland to Texas to find her and now that he had, he wasn't certain if life hadn't once again managed to turn happiness into a cruel joke.

Las Vegas, that evening

THE HAPPY CHAPEL of Wedded Bliss was located on the Strip, half a block from the Mirage Hotel. Sam and Duncan sat quietly in the waiting room while the dulcet tones of Wayne Newton singing "Hawaiian Wedding Song" filled the air.

Sam tried very hard not to notice the Elvis impersonator who was strutting his stuff to the amusement of the other couples awaiting their turn to enter the Love Room. The Love Room, they'd been informed, was where the actual wedding ceremonies took place. "Tastefully decorated in flocked velvet wallpaper and plush carpeting," the brochure proclaimed. "Why settle for second best?" As far as Sam was concerned, the only thing missing was a framed portrait of the poker-playing dogs.

Duncan had had little to say since they left Houston. It was late afternoon by the time they'd finished at the attorney's office, which left Sam only a few hours to tie up loose ends and pack for her new life. She'd purchased the condo furnished and had had nei-

ther the time nor the inclination to add her own personal touches.

For as long as she could remember, work had been
her life. Home was the place she went to when the
office was closed. Once they announced their elope-
ment, she would get on the telephone with her assistant and arrange to have her files shipped to Glenraven. Duncan had listened to her as she outlined her
plans then asked about who would ship her clothes.
"Ship them?" She'd laughed out loud at the thought.
"I can get everything I own in two suitcases."

The two suitcases were already checked through at
the airport for their flight to London.

Next to her, Duncan shifted position and glanced
at the clock.

"We still have time," Sam said. "Our flight
doesn't leave for another two hours."

One of the Happy Chapel's cheerful assistants
bounded over to them. The name *Lisa* was embroidered on the breast pocket of her hot pink blazer.
"Now you two are the Wilde-Stewart wedding,
right?"

"Aye," said Duncan, looking as if he wished he
were any place but where he was.

"Ooh," said the assistant. "An accent! Are you
Irish?"

Duncan's scowl deepened and Sam jumped in.
"He's from Scotland," she said quickly. "Can you
tell us how much longer the wait will be?"

"Oh, we have plenty of time," Lisa chirped.
"Now, you two bought the Standard Happy Chapel
package that comes with one photo." She eyed them
up and down. "Such a handsome couple! You really

should consider upgrading to the Ultra-Deluxe Happy Chapel package. It comes with five eight-by-ten color glossies to help you remember this special day.''

Sam hesitated. It might be nice to have pictures to show their child when he or she was older. She looked toward Duncan.

''No,'' he said, jaw set in a rock-hard line.

''Maybe we—''

''No.'' His tone brooked no argument and Sam, for once in her life, backed off. She felt as if he'd tossed cold water in her face.

This isn't a real marriage, Sam. Whatever else you do, don't forget that fact.

''He's right,'' she said. ''No pictures.''

Lisa, however, wasn't about to give up that easily. ''We have our Happy Chapel Honeymooners package. Only two photos but we add one wonderful night at the Mirage.'' She paused for effect. ''And tickets to see Siegfried and Roy.''

''We're happy with our choice,'' Sam said.

''We're happy,'' Duncan agreed.

From the look on Lisa's face, it was obvious she didn't believe a word of it and Sam couldn't blame her. They must look like they were about to face the executioner rather than Reverend Bob, Las Vegas's Marryingest Minister.

They sat in silence for what seemed an eternity until Duncan again checked his watch. ''Our flight leaves at midnight,'' he said.

''We have time,'' Sam said. ''The airport's not more than ten minutes away.''

That seemed to be Lisa's cue to join them once again. ''You're next,'' she announced, beaming at them like a happy bride herself. "Now you didn't want the Elvis package, did you?"

Both Sam and Duncan shook their heads.

"Okey-dokey," Lisa said, checking off something on her clipboard. "Then we're ready for you right now."

They didn't hold hands as they followed Lisa down a plushly carpeted hallway toward an enormous pair of brass double doors.

"Now you wait here just a sec," Lisa said. "We want to get the music cued."

A second later the strains of the "Wedding March" filled the air as Lisa returned with a small nosegay of flowers.

"Sorry," Lisa said with a shrug. "If you'd like to upgrade to the Happy Couple package, I can give you a stunning bouquet."

"This is fine," Sam said stiffly. "It's lovely."

"Well, then," said Lisa, "I'd say it's time for the ceremony to begin."

Reverend Bob was waiting for them at the glitter-dusted altar. He was a round little man with a Santa Claus beard and wide professional smile. Sam disliked him on sight.

"The happy bride and bridegroom," he boomed. "Step right up."

For a split second, Sam considered cutting her losses and running for her life. Anything had to be better than this travesty. She looked at Duncan's serious face and wondered if he was thinking the same thing.

They took their places as Lisa introduced them to Mary and Art, their two witnesses. Mary was a pleasant-faced woman in her mid-forties. Art looked like her male twin. Duncan nodded at the couple but didn't smile. Sam tried very hard to smile but failed miserably.

Reverend Bob said something but all Sam could hear was the sound of her heart thundering inside her chest. *This is for the rest of your life, Sam. Forever.* She realized Reverend Bob was waiting for her to say something.

"I'm sorry," she murmured. "Could you possibly—?"

The reverend's eyebrows shot up toward his receding hairline. The witnesses exchanged glances. Duncan, however, continued to look straight ahead.

Reverend Bob intoned the vows again and this time Sam parroted them perfectly. Then it was Duncan's turn. He sailed through the drill flawlessly.

"The ring?" asked Reverend Bob.

Duncan's eyes met Sam's.

"The ring," he said.

Sam nodded. "We forgot the ring."

"We have rings," the female witness piped up. "Four hundred dollars for a nice gold band, but if you're looking for something special, we can offer—"

"We'll use this." Duncan removed the heavy signet ring from his right hand.

Sam's fingers trembled as he easily slid the ring onto the middle finger of her left hand.

The Reverend looked dismayed. "I'm sure we have something that will fit the bride better than that."

"It's fine," Sam said, covering the ring with her other hand. "Go on with the ceremony."

"Now where was I?" the Reverend muttered, flipping through his little book. "Oh, yes. By the power invested in me by the state of Nevada, it is my pleasure and privilege to pronounce you two fine young people husband and wife." He looked at them and burst into laughter. "So what are you waiting for?" he said to Duncan. "You're entitled to one photo with your wedding package. Kiss your beautiful bride!"

"You don't have to do this," Sam murmured so only Duncan could hear.

"I know that," he said. "This is for posterity."

She understood immediately. He placed his hands on her waist. She rested her palms lightly against his chest. He lowered his head. She raised hers. His mouth brushed hers, gently at first, then with more insistent pressure. Her lips parted and he deepened the kiss. She could taste the wine they'd had at dinner and, for an instant, she wished this could be a real ceremony, with her family gathered around her instead of strangers, and that their first kiss could have been given in love and happiness.

"Wonderful!" cried the photographer as the quick flare of a flashbulb captured the moment.

Duncan abruptly broke the kiss and looked at his watch. "We'd better get to the airport."

"You're right," Sam said, as reality crashed down on her. "We don't want to miss our plane."

It was good to be reminded that hadn't been a real kiss any more than this was a real marriage.

"SIR?" The flight attendant stopped next to Duncan's seat. "Would your wife like an extra blanket?"

Duncan stared blankly at the pleasant young woman.

"Your wife," she repeated, grinning at him. "Would she like an extra blanket?"

"Yes," he said, his face reddening with embarrassment. "Thank you."

The flight attendant handed him a neatly folded blue blanket and a postage-stamp size pillow. "Newlyweds?" she asked.

He nodded. "We are."

"How long?"

He looked at his watch and she laughed.

"That long, huh?" She waggled her left hand and he saw the glint of light flashing off her diamond ring. "I take the plunge in October."

He wished her luck and she went off to see to the other passengers in first class. He turned to look at Sam, who was curled in the seat next to him, deeply asleep. She slept small, her long arms and legs pulled in close to her slender body, as if she was afraid to take up too much space. During takeoff, she'd hung on to his hand as if it was a lifeline, and he'd wondered how she'd survive the four and a half hour trip to New Jersey where they were scheduled to change planes. Exhaustion, however, had overcome her fears and she fell asleep before they reached cruising altitude.

What was it about her that touched him so deeply that his heart ached from it? There was a deep core of loneliness in his new bride that matched the loneliness inside his own heart, but that did not explain the depth of feeling she brought out in him. He told himself it was enough they shared the same dreams for their unborn child and were willing to do what was necessary to give that child a happy life, but he knew that was only part of the puzzle.

There was her strength and her determination, the soft uncertainty that lurked behind the steel. The woman behind the mask. He knew he could love that woman with his heart and soul.

And he prayed to God he never would.

THEY LANDED at Newark around eight in the morning. Their connecting flight to Gatwick was delayed and so they spent an hour in the VIP lounge, sipping orange juice and trying to make conversation. Sam felt groggy and out of sorts. Her stomach was queasy and twice she had to excuse herself to visit the ladies' room.

When she came back the second time, he was standing up with her overnight bag in his hand.

"The flight won't be leaving until evening, lassie."

Sam groaned. "You mean we'll be spending the day here?"

"I found us a hotel room next door."

"A room?" A faint alarm went through her. "I was only joking, Duncan. I can amuse myself here. I love airports."

"You can't sleep here."

"Who needs to sleep? I napped on the plane from Vegas."

"But I did not."

Suddenly she took a good look at her new husband and saw the dark circles beneath his eyes and she felt instantly guilty. "I'm sorry," she said. "I wasn't thinking."

He nodded but said nothing. In silence they made their way through the terminal, then hopped a shuttle bus for the adjacent hotel. How could she have missed the exhaustion on his face? It must be days since he'd had any sleep. The wonder was that he'd managed to make it this far without falling flat on his face.

They checked in at the front desk, then a bellman showed them to their room. Duncan reached into his pocket and pressed a bill into the man's outstretched hand, and a moment later the door clicked shut behind him. Sam set both locks then added the chain for good measure.

The room was small with nothing but the basics. A nightstand. A chest of drawers. A bed.

It was the bed that held her attention.

"Well," she said with false cheer, "why don't you wash up while I wait?"

He shook his head. "I'll wait," he said. "You first, lassie."

They hadn't been married long but already she knew that tone of voice brooked no argument. She picked up her overnight bag and disappeared into the small, well-lighted bathroom.

She looked terrible. Her face was pale and drawn tight as a drum, making her eyes look enormous, like the eyes in one of those paintings people laughed about. Her hair was tangled and messy. And her clothes looked slept in which, indeed, they had been. She unbuttoned her skirt, sighing with relief to discover she could actually breathe again. At least now she knew why all her clothing seemed as if it had been made for someone else.

She hung her skirt over the shower rod then removed her blouse and draped it over the skirt. Quickly she washed off her makeup, then dried her face on one of the scratchy blue towels stacked over the commode. The sharp smell of detergent made her stomach lurch, and it took her a second to recover. She prayed her luck would hold for the rest of her pregnancy.

"Now what?" she mumbled. She didn't have a nightgown with her, and she certainly couldn't sleep in her clothes. Strutting around in just her bra and slip seemed strange, so she slipped her blouse back on then opened the bathroom door and stepped into the darkened bedroom. "Duncan, the bathroom's yours—"

She stopped as her eyes adjusted to the lack of light. He was sprawled at an angle across the bed, his large frame claiming most of the queen-size mattress. Quietly she walked to the far side and stood near the edge of the bed, looking down at the man she'd married less than twelve hours ago.

He slept angrily. His brows were knotted in a scowl, creating furrows above the bridge of his nose. His hands were clenched at his sides, as if he was ready to leap up and do battle at a moment's notice. Most people betrayed vulnerability in their sleep, but not Duncan Stewart. Suddenly the enormity of what she'd done hit her full force and she sank onto the mattress before her trembling legs gave way.

This stranger who lay sleeping next to her was her husband. From this moment on, whenever she turned over in bed, she would see him there. One day the sight of him asleep would become commonplace, the same as the sight of her own face in the mirror, but

128 *Operation: Baby*

right now she found that impossible to believe. How would she ever get used to him if she never really got to know him?

And how could she get to know him when that wasn't part of the deal?

Chapter Eight

Castle Glenraven was set prominently at the top of a jagged hill, looking out toward the sea. Heavy white clouds swirled about the turrets, softening the hard stone edges and making the castle seem like something out of a fairy tale. One thousand years of Frasers and Stewarts had looked out upon that sea and gazed toward those mountains. One thousand years of Frasers and Stewarts had trod the stone walkway and picked berries from the low-hanging branches of blaeberry and ling.

Sam was stunned into silence as they approached the long, steep drive.

"My God," she said after a moment. "You live in a castle."

"You dinna know that, lass?" he asked, as he downshifted.

"There's knowing it and then there's knowing it," she said, shaking her head in utter disbelief. "I mean, I'm going to be living in a real castle." Her baby would not only grow up within the castle walls but one day all of this would belong to him or her. Houston seemed very far away. "How on earth do you heat it?"

"We don't."

"You're joking."

"We don't heat it in the American sense." They had fireplaces and room heaters and woodstoves but no central system. "Most of the rooms are closed off."

"Oh." She had a sudden vision of the two of them huddled around the kitchen table, warming their hands at the stove. "Do we— I mean, how many rooms are livable?"

"Not that many," he said, turning left onto the rutted uphill path. "Thirty or thirty-five at last count."

"Duncan, I've stayed in *hotels* with fewer rooms."

His smile was so quick she might have imagined it, but she didn't imagine the way it made her feel. When it came to her new husband, her emotions were all over the place and they were always intense.

"Your father's home is large," he pointed out.

"I thought it was until now. Fifteen rooms sound downright puny."

He told her something about this place, his heart's home, and she found herself listening with her own heart, as well. How could she not when he spoke with such passion and love. In the tenth century, the castle had been almost a city in itself. High stone walls had separated it from the rest of the countryside to the east. The deep wide sea formed a barrier to the west. He made her see the lives that had been lived behind those vanished walls. The coopers and the crofters, the wet nurses and warriors, the people who were his ancestors—they were all there, standing in front of her with their arms outstretched in welcome.

And now their child would take his or her place in line. This child would know he was loved. This child would have both parents by her side. This child would know a sense of security that neither Sam nor Duncan had ever enjoyed.

All Sam had to do was hang on to that thought and she'd be able to handle anything that came along.

Minutes later Duncan brought the car to a stop at what apparently served as the front door to the castle. Before he had a chance to walk around to her side of the car to open the door, a little berry of a woman flew out, her huge white apron billowing around her like a bridal gown.

If fury had a form, it was that fierce little woman as she stared at Duncan with blood in her eye. "It's a fine thing when I hear about it from the Widow Campbell before I hear it from the likes of you. I told the daft one she'd gone away with the fairies and yet here you be." She turned her fiery-eyed glare in Sam's direction.

Old Mag? Sam felt her stomach clench with apprehension. This was hardly the kind and loving housekeeper she'd envisioned.

"Come in, come in," Old Mag ordered, bustling around to Sam's side of the car. "The wind's high, 'twill be rainin' before long." Duncan moved toward Sam, but Mag would have none of it. "Out with you," she said to Sam. "You can't be doin' harm to the baby."

Sam froze in her seat. Duncan's face faded three shades to a ghostly white.

"It's finally happened," he said after he recovered his poise. "You're the one who's away with the fairies."

"Ach," Old Mag spat, holding out her hand to Sam. "I know what I know." She had the grip of a strong young man as she helped Sam from the car. "I see what's there before it comes to be."

"Rubbish," Duncan said. He'd regained some of his color, Sam noted. "If you have the gift, why didn't you know we were coming?"

"I know what's important," Old Mag said, studying Sam from head to foot. "You'll have a boy."

Sam's hands went to her belly instinctively, although she admitted nothing. "A boy?"

"Aye, there is no doubt. The look is in your eye."

"Well," said Sam, "that's quite a statement to make."

Old Mag's fiery gaze met her eyes. "You're a bonnie lass, as well, and that comes as no surprise."

"Th-thank you," Sam managed. "I'm Samantha."

"Old Mag to you." She motioned for Sam to bend down close. "Be good to him, lass," she whispered, "or you'll know the back of my hand. I'll not see him suffer like—"

"Enough, old woman," Duncan roared as he took their bags from the trunk. "Is the supper ready? Tell Robby to start a fire in the library."

Old Mag muttered something Sam couldn't even pretend to understand, then flew into the house in a swirl of white apron and long black skirt.

"Weren't you a little rough on her?" Sam asked as they started up the flower-lined pathway to the door.

"'Tis our way," he said.

"You can't blame her for being surprised, Duncan. I mean, *I'm* still surprised we're married, so you can imagine how she must be feeling."

"Tell me that this time next week after she's made your life a living hell."

"A living hell?" She forced a laugh. "I'm sure you're exaggerating."

The look he gave her made her wonder. "Old Mag has the heart of a lioness and the claws to match. Take care with her and you'll do well."

"You make it sound like I'll need a whip and a chair," Sam muttered.

His laughter surprised her. "No whip or chair," he said. "Just keep your wits and you'll be fine."

Sam felt an unexpected pang of disappointment as she crossed the threshold and stepped inside. Not that she'd been expecting anything in particular, but you'd have to have been raised on another planet to miss the significance of a brand-new bride, a brand-new groom and a threshold. Duncan, however, seemed oblivious to it all. He dropped their bags in the hall and bellowed, "Robby!" at the top of his lungs.

Sam winced and clapped her hands over her ears. "You'll wake the dead."

"Good," he said, "then maybe the man will hear me."

No sooner were the words out of his mouth than a tall white-haired man strolled down the hallway toward them. Sam had seen scarecrows with more meat on them. She almost swore she could hear his bones clacking together as he walked. The scarecrow looked at Sam, and his smile was so big and bright she found herself smiling back at him.

"Aye, a bonnie lass you are," the man said, with a nod toward Duncan. "As if he'd be bringin' home anything less."

In Texas a comment like that would have prompted her to start World War Three, but somehow, in this place, she found herself charmed. Even if the comment did make her feel like a prize trout. "Thank you," she said, extending her right hand. "I'm Sam."

The man took her hand in his as if it were made of the most delicate, translucent porcelain. "Robby Graham, and if ever you need something done, I'm the man to call." He said it with the rapt expression of a man declaring his undying love.

Sam was so touched she almost wept. "I'll remember that, Robby," she said, gently extricating her hand from his. "I'm very glad to meet you."

Robby's smile stretched so wide, she wondered it didn't split his face in two. "You're what we've needed," he said. "Not like the other one—"

Duncan stepped between the two of them. "The library," he said. "We need a fire."

Robby nodded, but his attentions were still focused on Sam. "A nasty one she was. Never time for so much as a—"

"Are you going to lay the fire, old man, or do I have to do it myself?"

"In a mood, he is," Robby said, not cowed in the least by Duncan's temper. "Been this way all his life if you ask me."

Sam did her best to hold back her laughter, but failed. Robby started to laugh, too, and she knew their friendship was sealed in mirth. Duncan, however, found no humor in the situation.

"You're a worthless man," he bellowed, picking up the suitcases and starting for the stairs. "It's a wonder I don't turn you out."

"You'd be lost without the likes of me," Robby said, with a wink for Sam. "I'll lay the fire for you, missus."

"He's wonderful," Sam said as Robby disappeared down the hallway.

"Ye think so because he's cow-eyed for you."

"I think so because he's delightful and has a sense of humor," she said, still grinning. "Which is more than I can say for you right now."

He didn't exactly smile, but Sam knew it was only a matter of time.

"Come with me," he said, "and I'll show you the living quarters."

She grabbed her tote bag and followed him down the corridor to a surprisingly elaborate staircase that led upstairs. The steps were wide and shallow, and it took her a second to find her rhythm. One day these steps would be as familiar to her as the elegantly carpeted steps of her town house. Right now, however, that seemed impossible to believe. Sights, sounds, smells—everything was strange to her. Her country's history would be nothing more than a footnote compared to the richness found in Duncan's lineage.

Dozens of portraits in ornate gold frames stared at her as she climbed the stairs. Women in Elizabethan dress. Men in ruffles and velvet. A parade of handsome young men in kilts with swords slung diagonally across their chests. She paused before a small oval portrait of a woman with hauntingly beautiful eyes, and a wave of the familiar dizziness washed over her.

"Lassie?" He was by her side in an instant. "What is it?"

"Nothing," she said. "I'm simply overwhelmed."

"You've gone pale."

His expression shifted for an instant, but before she could identify the emotion in his eyes, he put down the bags and swept her into his arms.

"I had no intention of fainting," she said.

"You had no intention of fainting the last two times, either."

He climbed the rest of the stairs with Sam cradled against his chest. "Do you plan on carrying me around until the baby is born?"

He pretended to stagger under her weight, and she laughed. It was these unexpected moments of connection between them that kept her so off balance.

They reached the landing, and instead of setting her on her feet, he carried her down the second floor hall, all the way to the last door on the left. The door was closed. She wondered if he just might carry her over this particular threshold, but he put her down then reached for the doorknob.

Wrong again, Sam. He's not going to carry you over this threshold or any other one. Get over it!

He swung open the door and motioned for her to step inside the room. She did and was instantly struck by the flood of light pouring in through the mullioned windows that lined two walls. The room was austere but no less beautiful for its simplicity, with lots of dark wood paneling, a chair and table near the far window, a bed the size of her office back home in Texas.

It dominated the room and her attention.

"Mag will unpack for you," Duncan said, placing Sam's big suitcase on the bed.

"What about your bags?"

"I take care of my own things."

"About the sleeping arrangements," she began. "I was wondering—"

"This is the master suite," he said. "The two fireplaces keep it warm in winter."

"I'm sure they do," she said, "but that's not—"

"The north side is windward. You don't want—"

"Damn it, Duncan, are you sleeping here, too?" She hadn't meant to say it with quite that sharp an edge, but there you had it.

"Where did you think I'd be sleeping?"

"I don't know. That's why I'm asking."

"This is my bed," he said. "This is where I sleep."

"Okay," she said, nodding. "I understand."

"I don't think you do, Samantha."

"We're married," she said, as if it was no big deal. "We sleep in the same bed. No problem."

He placed the palm of his hand against her belly and she thought she would go up in flames from his touch. "That's mine," he said in a low and thrilling voice. "We made that together."

"I know," she said, her voice suddenly husky. She felt herself swaying toward him, melting like a quick-burning candle. *It was like this that first time*, she thought. *So fast. So crazy.*

He cupped her buttocks in his hands and pulled her

close to him, fitting himself against her. He was rock-hard. She could feel his heat burning through their clothes.

"We're married," he said, moving his hands over her hips, her waist, her rib cage. "Is this part of the bargain?"

"I don't know," she said. "Is it?"

"That's for you to decide, lassie." He released her and took a step backward. "You set the boundaries."

He sounded so businesslike, as if he could turn on and off again at will.

"Maybe we should have had our lawyers work out the details for us," she snapped, stung by his abrupt change of attitude.

"What happens in our bedroom is nobody's business but ours."

"And what if nothing happens in our bedroom?" she countered, unable to control her voice.

"Then that is your decision," he said evenly, not rising to her bait.

"You could live with that?"

"You draw the boundaries, lassie, and I will live within them or without them as I choose."

"Fine," she said. "I'll do that."

"We'll love the child," he said. "We canna ask more from marriage than that."

She knew he was wrong but couldn't find the words to tell him how or why.

They stood there in awkward silence for a few moments. Sam vowed it would take an act of God to get her to speak first.

Duncan cleared his throat. "Would you like to see the other rooms on this floor?"

"Thank you," Sam said, "but maybe some other time."

She could almost see the dark storm clouds gather over his head. "You can find your way downstairs?"

"I think I can manage."

He turned and left the room without another word.

Sam considered going after him and apologizing for her sharp tongue but sheer stubbornness held her back. She hadn't insulted him or his country or violated any international laws. All she'd done was refuse an offer to explore her new home. Considering the fact that this would be her home for the rest of her life, there'd be plenty of other opportunities.

Why not go for broke, she thought, looking at the suitcases stacked on the bed. If she unpacked her own clothing, she could dig herself an even deeper hole with Mag—if that was humanly possible. The old woman's whispered threat still echoed in her ears. *Be good to him, lass, or you'll know the back of my hand. I'll not see him suffer like—*

Like what? Like he suffered the last time he had a cold? She knew that couldn't possibly be what Mag was hinting at. No, it had something to do with a woman. And she'd almost be willing to bet her stake in Wilde & Daughters Ltd. that it was his ex-wife who'd made him suffer.

AN HOUR LATER Sam joined Duncan in the library for supper. Mag had set up a card table in front of the fire and laid it with a dark green cloth and the best china and silver.

"She hates me," Sam said as Mag and Robby left the room. "Did you see the way she threw my food at me?'' One of the roasted new potatoes had bounced off Sam's plate and rolled under her chair.

"She doesn't know you, lass," he said. "How can she hate you?"

"I unpacked my own things." She pierced a carrot with her fork then popped it into her mouth. "That's one reason."

"I told you she'd take care of it."

"It wasn't a difficult task, Duncan," she said tartly. "Besides, that's only the half of it. She also doesn't think I'm good enough for you."

The furrow between his eyes deepened. "She said that to you?"

"She didn't have to say anything. It's the way she looks at me."

"Old Mag looks the way she looks. 'Tis nothing unusual."

"She probably thinks you should have married a Scotswoman."

"Aye," he agreed, "she would think that."

"And she's probably scandalized that I'm already pregnant."

"She doesn't know that."

"She knows." Sam's laugh was brittle. "I don't know how she knows, but she has it all figured out."

"You read too much into an old woman's ways," he said, but there was something in his voice that piqued her curiosity. "She hasn't the gift of second sight, if that's what you're asking."

"That's not what I'm asking."

He pushed back his chair and stood abruptly.

"Duncan?" she asked. "What is it?"

"Don't worry," he said. "I'll take care of Mag."
Before she could protest, he left the room.

SAM FINISHED her supper then curled up in her chair
to watch the fire dance in the hearth. She had no idea
where Duncan had disappeared to, and for the moment, she was just as glad. He'd been gone for the
better part of an hour with not so much as a word of
explanation. She'd heard Old Mag's voice in the hallway, but it was Robby who cleared away the trays
and brought Sam a pot of tea and some shortbread.
He positively beamed with pleasure as he poured the
dark brew. It was nice to know someone in the castle
liked her.

When you came down to it, she had no idea at all
if her husband did. In truth, how could he, when he
didn't know her any better than she knew him. She
didn't know his birthday, his favorite foods, what
kind of music made him feel like dancing. Or if he
danced at all. Was he kind to animals and small children? Would he care if she told him she had no idea
what she was supposed to do with her life now that
she was queen of the castle? Once the baby came, her
role would be more clearly defined, but right now she
felt downright rudderless.

She poured herself another cup of tea and drew her
chair closer to the fire. Back home in Houston she'd
be wearing shorts and a tank top, wondering if it was
time to turn on the central air-conditioning. Home,
she thought. Houston wasn't home anymore, was it?
Glenraven was her home now, as it was her husband's
home, and would be their child's home, as well. She
waited for the word to resonate inside her heart, but
that sense of rightness never came.

Maybe it never would. It wasn't as if she'd ever felt a deep spiritual connection to the place where she was born. Oh, sure, she had the same loyalty all Texans had for their home state, but that overwhelming sense of pride and belonging had somehow eluded her, as if she had been waiting all this time to find out where she was meant to be. Was this wild and beautiful place what she'd been searching for?

She glanced around the library and found nothing of herself anywhere she looked. The books were strange to her, beautiful old leather volumes of poetry and history and art that smelled like salt air and heather. The photographs on the desk were of people she'd never met. The needlepoint cushions featured a coat of arms that had nothing at all to do with her.

A rush of anger brought her up short. Why wasn't Duncan there with her, helping her settle in? This was worse than being stood up for the high school prom by Cal Hutchens. At least then she'd been able to run upstairs to her own room and slam the door closed on the world. Here, she was expected to sleep with him.

She glanced at her watch, which had been reset to local time. Nearly nine o'clock. That wasn't too early for a pregnant woman to go to bed. If she hurried, maybe she could bathe, brush her teeth and be sound asleep before he joined her.

It was the coward's way out but it was the best she could do tonight.

Chapter Nine

Duncan stood by the window of his studio and stared at the castle. An open bottle of Glenraven's best rested on the sill. He'd watched the lights go off one by one until the only light remaining was the one in his room. He wondered what she was doing, what mysterious female nighttime ritual she was performing.

This stranger, his wife.

He imagined her rising from her bath, a cloud of perfumed steam billowing about her knees and thighs. He could see droplets of water sliding down the curve of her belly, down the sleek line of her thighs. He could see himself dropping to his knees in front of her and capturing those drops of water with the tip of his tongue. She would taste warm and sweet and female and he—

Whiskey was a poor substitute for a woman's body, he thought, as he lifted the bottle to his mouth and drank. That sweet, soft welcome for which men fought wars. He hadn't been with a woman since Samantha. Not since that afternoon in the spring rain when he'd come closer to heaven than any man had the right to. She'd branded him, and he'd not been the same since.

And she would probably never know.

That was the one thing they hadn't provided for in the endless reams of paper detailing the specifics of their marriage.

She had his heart. She'd had it from the first moment when she came to his arms beside the loch.

He saw the faintest shadow of movement behind the curtains in his room. A willowy figure paused for a moment, silhouetted by the bedroom lamp, then disappeared from view. But not from his memory. He remembered too well how she'd felt in his arms, the way her slender body had accommodated itself to him, how perfectly they'd fit together. And more than that, he remembered the way she'd made him feel.

He turned from the window and polished off the last of the single malt, but nothing dulled the sharp stab of hunger deep in the pit of his belly.

A man had the right to sleep in his own bed, but that fact somehow didn't wash with the look he'd seen in his wife's eyes. She feared him—or was it herself she feared? He didn't know why that thought came to him. It must be the whiskey speaking. Whiskey made a man wonder about things that were no concern of his. The lives they'd led before no longer mattered. Wasn't that what they'd said in those endless pages of legal documents that passed for commitment these days? The child was what mattered, making certain he or she was cradled in the secure arms of a mother and father who would always be there.

But it wasn't the child he thought about now.

It was the woman.

DUNCAN HAD certainly spared no expense when it came to remodeling the master bath, Sam thought as she climbed from the enormous sunken tub and reached for a towel. She sighed with pleasure as she wrapped the warm bath sheet around her damp body. A heated towel rack—now there was a great invention for you. She wondered if Duncan had thought to add that particular touch or if some high-priced interior designer had come up with it.

Not that it mattered, she told herself as she quickly blew dry her hair. He was a decidedly sensual man. All you had to do was take one look at his sculptures and there could be no doubt of that. He understood the shape and flow of the human body in a way that was carnal but somehow never crossed over into being lewd.

She knew little of the man but had absorbed the artist through her eyes and skin. His touch was everywhere she looked in the room. The nubby texture of the curtains, the rough wood paneling, the blazing fireplace smelling of heather and pine. She pressed a second towel to her face and breathed deeply, imagining she caught the scent of his skin in the warm fabric and then realized what she was doing and dropped the towel to the floor.

She dried off quickly, then folded both towels and placed them on the bench next to the tub. Her nightgown was still draped across the foot of the bed in the other room. She hated to leave the humid warmth of the bathroom, but the quicker she slipped on her nightgown, the quicker she could slip into bed and be sound asleep when—or if—Duncan came to join her.

She swung open the door and found herself face-to-face with her husband.

"Duncan!" Her voice was high with surprise. "I didn't—" Her words died in her throat as she saw the look in his eyes. She wanted to step back into the safe womb of the bath or at least make an attempt to cover herself, but she couldn't move beneath the heavy measure of his gaze.

Everything Duncan was or had ever dreamed of being faded before the radiance of his new wife's naked body. She glowed with some inner light, as if the power and glory of the moon had found its center within her soul.

He wanted to tell her she was beautiful but he was afraid he would say that and more. She stood perfectly still, her arms at her sides, and she didn't turn away. Her skin shimmered in the firelight, a smooth expanse of finest marble made warmly human by the kiss of the gods. Her breasts were larger than he'd remembered them, the areolae and nipples dark rose and tempting. Her hair fell softly across her shoulders, a shimmering mantle of gold. And her belly, that glorious round swell—

Her voice came to him through a fog of desire. He wondered how long she'd been talking to him.

"Duncan, would you *please* hand me my nightgown?"

A swath of ivory silk lay curled at the foot of the bed. He picked it up between thumb and forefinger and handed it to her. The faint scent of her perfume lingered in the air around him.

"Thank you," she murmured then raised her long, lovely arms overhead and let the nightgown slither its way down her body.

It seemed a crime to cover her nakedness, he thought. She was perfect in every way a woman could be perfect—and possibly in a few ways unique to her.

The gown caressed her breasts and accentuated the womanly swell of her belly. It suggested more than it revealed and, overall, the effect it had on him was nearly as powerful as her unexpected nakedness. If she knew this, she gave no indication. She carried herself with an air of reserve that touched his heart even as it puzzled him.

She stood at the foot of the bed and met his eyes. "Which side would you like?" she asked, her tone formal and polite.

"I dinna care," he said truthfully. "'Tis your choice, lassie."

Her cheeks reddened and she walked to the far side of the bed and carefully turned down the spread. "This will be fine," she said, "if you have no objection."

"I have none." He watched as she sat on the edge of the mattress then removed her watch and placed it on the end table. She swung her long slender legs onto the bed then quickly pulled the covers up to her shoulders. "You're going to sleep early," he observed.

"Yes," she said, still stiff and formal. "The doctor said I should get as much sleep as I possibly can."

He nodded and turned away. "Then I'll leave you to your rest, Samantha." It was only then that he realized in her bedtime ritual she hadn't removed his ring.

SAM LAY AWAKE in the darkness for what seemed like hours.

This is what you wanted, she told herself. *A big wide bed with nobody in it but you.*

She could somersault from one side of the bed to the other and have room to spare. Certainly she was in no danger of bumping into Duncan. She could still hear the sound of his footsteps disappearing down the hallway. There'd been something almost final about the sound, as if some last piece of a puzzle had finally snapped into place, revealing the whole for everyone on earth to see except Sam.

She'd come so close to calling him back. What would it have taken, really? Two or three words at the most and he would be by her side right now. She could have been in his arms, cradled against his big broad chest, listening to the rhythm of his heartbeat instead of her own.

But that wasn't part of the deal, she told herself. If she started looking for emotional attachments where there were none, she'd only be setting herself up for a terrible fall. Besides, she had something much more important to think about than her own foolish heart. She had the baby to consider and the safe and secure future that had made this marriage of convenience sound like such a wonderful idea in the first place.

Better she learned to accept the way things were and not waste time or energy dreaming about some impossible romantic ideal that, up until this pregnancy, hadn't been part of her vocabulary. Once the baby came and her hormones returned to something approximating normal, then she'd be her old self again. Practical, down-to-earth, and about as romantic as a pair of old shoes.

She groaned and buried her face deep in her pillow. Until then, she'd just have to suffer.

IT WAS PAST TWO when Duncan came to bed after spending some long and unproductive hours alone in his studio. He moved quietly about the room, retrieving various items from his overnight bag, careful not to wake his sleeping bride. He took a long, hot shower, letting the water pound mercilessly on the knotted muscles of his back and shoulders, but to little effect. It would take more than water to release the tension coiled inside him.

The castle was different with her in it. In the space of a few hours, she'd somehow managed to turn his familiar surroundings into a place he no longer recognized, and she had done it without changing a thing. He felt disoriented and strangely exhilarated, as if he'd returned from a long journey to find someone else there living his old life.

He showered until the hot water ran out then toweled off with greater care than usual. Even brushing his teeth seemed to require more attention. Finally he ran out of ways to delay the inevitable. The time had come to climb into bed next to his radiantly beautiful wife and pretend he didn't want her with his entire heart and soul.

He switched off the bathroom light, then opened the door. The faintest shimmer of moonlight filtered through a crack in the drapes, just enough so that he could make out the slender line of her leg where the cover had fallen away. Something stirred deep inside him, deeper even than the drumbeat of blood. He wanted more than to make love to her. He wanted to gather her close to him and keep her from harm.

And those feelings of tenderness did more to scare him than lust ever could.

HE THOUGHT she was asleep.

Sam lay perfectly still as he moved about the room. She'd been wide awake from the moment he first came upstairs. She'd lain there, rigidly still, while he'd stripped off his clothes, then while he took the world's longest hot shower. The smells of steam and soap still perfumed the cool air of their bedroom.

There was something endearing about his stealth. He was obviously trying his best to keep from disturbing her, and his concern touched her. She held her breath as he turned down the covers on his side of the bed. The mattress dipped when he climbed in then shifted again as he settled beneath the sheet and blanket. It didn't take a great leap of imagination to figure out that he was probably stark naked over there. If ever a man wasn't the pajama type, it was Duncan.

Not that it mattered. Naked or clothed, it made no difference to her.

And maybe if she told that to herself another hundred times, she might begin to believe it.

He shifted position twice. Each time he did, she had to grip the blanket tightly to keep from sliding across the mattress toward him. She heard his low exhalation of breath as he punched his pillow into place, and her entire body was galvanized by the sound. Her heartbeat accelerated and she felt the way she had the first time he kissed her.

At this rate she wouldn't survive their first week of married life.

SAM'S DREAMS that night were a wild Technicolor splash of erotic images that seemed to spring from some hidden corner of her heart, a place she'd never known existed until now. She felt Duncan's hands skimming her body, caressing her hips, the inward curve of her waist, the flare of her rib cage. She felt his weight pressing her deeper into the soft mattress, the way he positioned his body between her thighs. She felt herself melting, opening, drawing him closer and closer until their bodies joined together in that ancient dance.

She could hear the sounds he made when he climaxed. She could smell herself on his skin. She could feel the delicious stretch of accommodation as her body fit itself around him. It was all so real, so wondrously real that when she awoke that morning, she was shocked to find herself alone.

The covers on Duncan's side of the bed were more or less back in place and except for the badly rumpled pillow, she couldn't have proven he'd been there at all. In a way she was glad he wasn't there. After the dreams she'd had, she would have had trouble facing him without blushing a fiery shade of red.

She reached for her watch on the nightstand. A few minutes after seven. She tried to figure out what time that would be in Houston but her brain refused to cooperate. Besides, Houston time wasn't an issue any longer, was it? She was in Scotland now, and it was time she made the adjustment.

She made her way downstairs a little while later. Her stomach felt a bit shaky, but so far it seemed to be nothing she couldn't handle. She'd been incredibly lucky so far when it came to morning sickness. If this unsettled feeling was the worst of it, she wouldn't question her good fortune.

She poked her head into the dining room. The table was highly polished but unset. She glanced at the sideboard. Nothing going on there, either. Lucky's housekeeper made sure breakfast was ready and waiting by seven every morning, come hell or tornadoes. Of course, this wasn't Texas. For all she knew, maybe she was supposed to make her own breakfast. She didn't know the first thing about castle etiquette, and Mag was the last one she'd ask.

She stepped into the dark hallway. She caught the faintest scent of bacon and followed her nose down the corridor to where it opened into a huge stone kitchen blessed with every shiny modern appliance you could imagine. A pot simmered on the back of the enormous stove. She lifted the lid and a blast of highly spiced steam rushed up at her. She dropped the lid and, hand over her mouth, made it out the back door just in the nick of time.

"Och," said a flinty voice behind her, "just as I thought. A baby is on its way."

Sam pushed her hair off her face and rose to her feet. "Yes," she said, not feeling terribly friendly. "Congratulations. You were right. You must be overjoyed."

The little crone reached out and placed a hand against Sam's flat belly. "Three months?"

"Almost," Sam said. She wanted to brush the woman's hand away but suppressed the urge.

"The sickness is a good thing."

"You couldn't prove it by me." She had hoped the worst of morning sickness would pass her by but apparently her luck had run out.

"Sickness means a healthy baby," Old Mag said, fixing Sam with one of those fierce-eyed stares.

"Isn't that an old wives' tale?"

"And what would you know about old wives," Mag countered, "being a new wife yourself?"

There was something comical about so much ferocity in such a tiny package, and to her dismay, Sam barely stifled a laugh.

"The other one wouldn't laugh if she swallowed a goose feather."

"The other one?"

"Aye, the first missus."

Sam had totally forgotten that this wasn't her husband's first marriage. Talk about denial.

"He told you about her, didn't he?" Old Mag asked.

"He told me he'd been married before." Which was true enough. A mistake, he'd said, and one they'd quickly rectified. She hadn't thought to pursue it. It didn't seem like any of her business.

"A coldhearted one, she was," Mag said. "Nearly broke his heart with her ways."

"I don't think you should be talking about this with me," Sam said. His past wasn't any business of hers. The old woman made it sound as if he'd been deeply in love with his first wife, and Sam found she didn't want to hear any of it.

"One look in those eyes and you knew she would not make him happy."

"You could tell just by looking at her?" *Let it drop, Sam. Don't encourage her. This is none of your business.*

"'Twas almost easy as knowing about your baby."

Sam couldn't deny that the woman had been right on that score.

Mag leaned a little closer. "When she found out that she—"

"Stop, old woman!" Robby burst into the room. His cheeks reddened as he nodded hello to Sam. "I'll have no sweetie wife of mine spreading stories."

Sam's eyes went wide with curiosity as the elderly man turned toward her and smiled.

"Morning, missus."

"Good morning, Robby." She glanced from Robby to Mag. "You two are married?"

Old Mag gave him a look of fond disgust. "As if anyone else would have him."

"You talk too much," Robby said to his wife in a tone of husbandly displeasure. "You don't have work to do?"

Mag said something quickly, in a burr so thick that Sam could understand none of it. Robby had no trouble, however, and he fired back a salvo of his own that set his wife to wagging her finger beneath his bony nose.

Sam listened, fascinated, as they exchanged words, wondering how on earth two such different personalities had managed to stay married. Robby, apparently content that he had prevented a disaster in the making, gave Sam a big smile then went off to do something in the garage. Sam followed Old Mag into the kitchen.

She stood near the door, waiting for some clue as to who was supposed to do what, but Old Mag buzzed about the room, paying her no mind at all. Finally Sam went over to the enormous stove and poured herself a cup of tea.

"Honey if you want it," the woman said, pushing a honey pot toward Sam.

"Thank you," Sam said, "but I don't use honey."

"Sugar, as well."

"I don't use that, either."

"You be needing to eat for the baby, lassie. You're too bony."

"I don't think upping my sugar intake is the way to do it."

Mag looked at her curiously. "Your tongue is sharp."

"So is yours," Sam returned.

"Aye," said Mag, nodding her head. "But few would tell me so."

"Not too many tell me so, either."

"That doesn't surprise me, lassie."

The two women looked at each other for what seemed an eternity before Sam spoke. "You know that bread you served with supper last night?"

"Aye," said Old Mag, "I would hope I did. I baked it myself."

"Do we have any more?" Sam asked. "I'd love to make some toast."

"Toast?" Mag made a face. "You need more than

toast to fill your stomach.'' She gestured toward the enormous table in the middle of the room. ''Sit down and let me fix you a proper breakfast.''

The thought of a proper breakfast was enough to make Sam's stomach turn inside out for the second time that morning, but there was no way she could refuse Old Mag's offer. Not if they were going to live together under the same roof.

''Thank you,'' she said, taking a seat at the table. ''That's very kind of you.''

''Not kind at all.'' Mag sniffed. ''You don't know your way about my kitchen. 'Tis faster this way.''

Which put Sam firmly in her place. Actually she found she didn't mind a bit. She'd rather know exactly how Mag felt about her than waste a lot of time worrying and guessing—then managing to do the wrong thing anyway.

The old woman worked quickly, and in record time Sam was presented with two perfectly toasted pieces of dark-grained bread, a crock of butter and some orange marmalade. Before she had the chance to finish the first slice, Mag placed a bowl of steaming oatmeal in front of her.

''Thank you,'' Sam said, ''but I couldn't possibly.''

''You could and you will,'' Mag said, pouring fresh milk into the bowl. ''Think of the baby, lassie.''

Sam shuddered. ''What if I—''

''It will not happen again today,'' Mag said with great confidence.

''How can you be so sure?''

''Eight babies of my own, all still living, is how I can be so sure.''

Sam's eyes nearly popped as she looked at the tiny slip of a woman who stood before her. "Eight!"

"Aye, and no birth took longer than six hours."

Sam considered her carefully. "And you ate oatmeal?"

Was that the beginning of a smile tugging at the corners of Old Mag's disapproving mouth? "Every morning."

Sam sighed and picked up her spoon. "Then who am I to argue with success?"

She dug in.

Chapter Ten

Sam ate what she could of the oatmeal under Old Mag's watchful eye. They said little to each other, but Sam sensed they'd turned a corner in the relationship and she was glad. It was obvious that the housekeeper would throw herself on a sword for Duncan, and Sam knew her life at the castle would be a great deal easier if she had the fierce old woman on her side.

Mag was busy paring potatoes when Sam finished the last of the cereal, so she washed her dishes then dried them and put them away in the cupboard.

"Thank you for breakfast," she said to Mag. "It was delicious."

"You don't have to wash up next time, lassie. 'Tis my job to do for you."

"A little work won't kill me," Sam said, smiling easily for the first time.

"You're a good one," Mag pronounced. "He chose well this time."

Sam took a deep breath and decided to plunge in. "That's the second time you've said something like that."

Mag looked away. "I'm an old woman. Sometimes my tongue runs away with me."

"Why did you dislike his first wife so much? What—"

"Robby calls me," Mag said, then hurried from the kitchen as if the hounds of hell were at her heels.

So much for discovering any of Duncan's secrets.

Sam went upstairs to brush her teeth and fix her makeup. And, she admitted to herself, to see if her husband might have returned to their bedroom. Unfortunately, everything was exactly the way she'd left it an hour ago. She straightened the bed, then sat by the window. It wasn't quite nine in the morning and the day stretched out in front of her, an endless string of empty hours waiting to be filled.

She could either spend them wondering about her husband's past or she could get on with building her new life. She didn't need to be told which was the better bet.

With a little luck, her work files would arrive by the end of the week, which meant she had to have someplace to store them. A work space, she thought. An office, even. She was living in a gazillion-room castle. It shouldn't be too terribly difficult to come up with a place where she could work.

She would have to ask Duncan to show her around and help her pick the best spot. Of course, to do that she'd have to find him first.

Sam went downstairs. She peeked into the library, the parlor and the dining room, then walked to the kitchen. Neither Old Mag nor Robby was anywhere to be seen. She stepped out the back door into the garden, where she discovered bed after bed of chervil and oregano and thyme and rosemary, among many others, all planted in neat rows on either side of the stone path. In another month or so, the scent would be downright heavenly.

She followed the path past a gardener's shed and what looked to be the remnants of some sort of arsenal. You could almost see the shimmer of history, like the mist curling up from the sea. Knowing that her child would be linked to all who had come before filled Sam with a sense of wonder she'd never known.

The path led past the garage, where Robby and two young men were busy doing something that required lots of power and equal amounts of noise. Sam waved at them and continued walking. She considered asking them if they'd seen Duncan anywhere but decided against it.

A small stone building, obviously modern, stood about one hundred yards away from the garage. It had a high, flat roof and enormous windows and looked as if it had been dropped on the castle grounds by mistake. She wondered if it was a guest house, although why you'd need a guest house when you owned a castle was beyond her.

She approached the building and tried to peer through one of the windows. The only thing she saw was her reflection peering back at her. Mirrored glass. Wouldn't you know it? She walked around the side of the building and found the same thing, and from there she went to the front where she was pleased to find the door was slightly ajar.

She didn't hesitate a second. She pushed it open then stepped inside and she instantly understood where she was.

Duncan's studio.

The room was awash in the purest light imaginable and all of it seemed to be centered on the man himself. Her chest felt tight as she looked at him. His shirtsleeves were rolled to the elbow, and her eye was drawn to the way the muscles of his forearms tensed each time he tapped hammer to chisel. Chips of marble glittered like diamonds in the sunlight as they flew up and away from his chisel.

She stood quietly by the door, scarcely breathing. So this was how magic happened, from hard muscular work and genius. She should have known. The earthy sensuality of his sculptures wasn't the result of some intellectual exercise. It was born in the body, of muscle and sinew and sweat, and those things are what gave it dimension.

A voluptuous shiver rippled through her as he shifted position. His chest and forearms glistened, and she found herself longing to draw the tip of her tongue along each swell of muscle.

"Step inside and close the door, lassie."

She jumped at the sound of his voice. "How did you know I was standing here?"

"Your perfume," he said.

Another shiver went through her as she shut the door.

"I didn't realize this was your studio," she said.

"Come closer," he said, drawing the back of his arm across his eyes.

"I'm fine right here."

"You're in my light, lassie."

In his light? That hardly seemed possible. The place was flooded with sun. Still, she moved deeper into the room, aware of the feel of her breasts beneath her sweater, of the unfamiliar sway of her hips with each step she took. She wondered if she would ever get used to her new, more womanly body or if she would spend the rest of her pregnancy feeling like a stranger in her own skin.

She stopped a few feet away from Duncan, who was still absorbed in his work. His concentration was almost palpable, like a force field that kept the rest of the world at bay. She wondered how it would feel to be the focus of all that intensity, to have him look at her that way, as if there was nothing and nobody else on earth that mattered.

The thought made her light-headed. She'd never inspired that kind of intensity in a man. There was certainly no reason to believe she'd ever inspire it in her new husband. She hadn't even been able to inspire him to spend the entire night in the same bed.

He drew the back of his arm across his eyes again, and the male grace of the gesture made her breath catch in her throat. Hormones, she told herself. In a few months she wouldn't even notice gestures like that.

He positioned the chisel once more and tapped the hammer against it, three times in rapid succession, then grimaced.

"What are you working on?" she asked. His body shielded the piece from her eyes.

He stepped away from the bench and wiped his hands on his thighs. "Look for yourself, lassie."

She approached cautiously, aware of his nearness, of the fact that this was so clearly his territory and his alone. A block of marble lay sideways across the table. It wasn't terribly impressive in size, certainly no more than two feet wide and half that deep. That was what she noticed first. The marble was a pale ivory color, tinted faintly yellow from the sunlight splashing across it. At first she saw nothing but angles and edges, and she felt a sharp stab of disappointment that his genius could seem so ordinary up close.

Then, suddenly, she focused in. Rising somehow from the marble itself was the gentle S curve of a woman's back and the suggestion of a strong jawline and long neck. A jolt of recognition shot through her and she looked at Duncan. "That's me," she said quietly. "Isn't it?"

"Aye," he said, "or it will be."

She bent low over the marble and ran the tip of her index finger along the curve. "I—I don't know what to say."

"Say nothing, lassie. Just stand there and let me capture the angle of your shoulders."

She wrapped her arms around her waist and stepped back. "You're joking."

The look in his eyes told her otherwise.

"I don't know the first thing about modeling."

"There is nothing you need to know." He placed his index finger under her chin and tilted her head. Then he angled her right shoulder down, down, until she felt the elongation of her spine, the shimmering S curve she'd seen rising from the marble. "Hold that...."

As if she could do anything else when he was looking at her that way.

The only sound in the room was the rhythmic tap of hammer to chisel. He circled the slab of marble, quickly etching a curve here, an angle there. His intensity was overwhelming. It seemed to draw the oxygen from her lungs.

Her nose itched but she held the pose steady. When her right arm began to tremble, she ignored it rather than disturb his concentration. However, when he gestured for her to turn to the left, she shook her head. "My leg's asleep," she said by way of apology. "If I turn, I'll fall over."

He dragged a chaise longue from the corner to the middle of the room then led her to it.

"I'm not a model, Duncan," she protested as he helped her swing her legs onto the chair. "This is crazy."

"A few more minutes," he said, positioning her body in the elongated sweep of his sculpture.

There was something highly provocative about the position but she couldn't say how or why. She was fully clothed. She wasn't touching herself in any way that might be deemed erotic. And yet she felt as if every muscle in her body was being primed somehow for the act of love. For sex in all its infinite variety and joy. Was that the secret to his art, then, this ability to translate the ordinary stuff of life into pure sizzle and burn? Whatever it was, she felt the heat move through her like wildfire.

She found herself relaxing, enjoying the sensation of being the focus of his concentration. There was something heady and exciting about it, to know that it was the sweep of her throat, the curve of her spine, that inspired him.

He stopped every so often and guided her gently into another position, subtle alterations of line and angle that seemed to trigger an artistic response from him. Magic was rising from that cold block of marble, and it thrilled her to be a part of it.

DUNCAN WORKED as swiftly as he could, trying to capture her line before she grew too tired. There was something endearing about her self-consciousness, and he found himself trying to convey that uncertainty beneath the sheer beauty of her physical form.

Because that was the miracle of it all. She was, in all ways, a goddess yet unaware of the extraordinary power granted to her. The early stages of pregnancy had softened her beauty, turned her slim-hipped, colt-ish quality into something womanly and deeply alluring. Clothes seemed an abomination. She should be proudly naked, her ripe beauty there to be worshiped by mere mortals.

He wondered what she would do if he asked her to strip off her clothes for him right then and there. He put down the hammer and chisel and moved toward her. She was so beautiful with the sunlight turning her pale hair to molten gold that he wished he could stop time and live in that moment forever.

"Is something wrong?" she asked as he drew close.

He shook his head. "Nothing," he said. "You're perfect."

Her eyes widened and she broke the pose. "Duncan, I—"

He placed his hands on her shoulders, feeling the delicate bone structure beneath his fingertips, letting that knowledge work its way into his subconscious. A tiny vein in her right temple pulsed wildly, and it

took all his self-control to keep from placing his lips
against the spot.

She tensed. He could feel the slightest trembling
and he murmured something low, something he didn't
expect her to understand, then moved his hands across
her shoulders and down her arms, stroking her. She
sighed, a softly sibilant sound, and he took it as encouragement. Gently he eased her sweater off her
right shoulder, exposing the smooth skin and exqui-
site line.

"Duncan?" She sounded both puzzled and
pleased.

"I need to see you," he said, then eased her
sweater off her left shoulder, as well.

She dipped her head, and her cascade of hair fell
across both shoulders.

"No," he said, gathering the silky fall into his
hands. "I want to see you." He resisted the urge to
bury his face against the fragrant mass.

She nodded then lowered the sweater farther, revealing the curving swell of her breasts. The gesture
touched him deeply, for he knew how difficult it was
for her.

"Aye," he said, "that's it." Although it was only
part of what he wanted from her. Still, it was more
than he'd thought he would find.

He picked up his hammer and chisel again, determined to find a way to turn mere marble into something worthy of her splendor. He wanted to see her
breasts revealed to his eyes, he wanted to see the
swell of her belly and know it cradled his child. He
wanted—

"Did you hear something?" she asked.

Only the sound of my heart, lassie. "I dinna think so."

"I'm sure I heard something, Duncan. Listen."

He did and quickly realized she was right. "There's someone at the door," he said.

She tugged her sweater into position. "Do you usually have visitors when you're working?"

He shook his head. "Never." He waited while she smoothed her hair then he went to open the door.

"Took you long enough!" Old Mag railed at him from the doorway. She glanced curiously at Samantha who smiled at her from the chaise longue. "There's a telephone call for you, missus."

Sam stood and smoothed her skirt. "A phone call?"

"Says she's your mother and that she needs to speak with you right now."

"That sounds like my mother," Sam said to Duncan. "I'd better take the call."

She hurried from the studio, and most of the light in the room seemed to vanish with her.

"And what are you looking at, old woman?" he asked Mag. "You don't have work of your own?"

"She does not love you yet, laddie, but she will in time."

He stared at her. "What in bloody hell does that mean?"

"It means give her time."

"You're talking nonsense, old woman. We're married."

"I have eyes to see with, don't think I don't, and this marriage isn't all it should be."

He hated when she did that, saw through his lies

to the heart of the matter. "This marriage is not your business," he said.

"Tell her, laddie. You might be surprised."

The only thing that surprised him was that Old Mag still had her position.

IT TOOK SAM a few minutes but she finally tracked down the telephone in the dining room, of all places.

"Tell me you're not married," Julia greeted her. "Tell me this letter is a terrible joke."

"Hello to you, too, Mother," she said, sitting down at the highly polished mahogany table. "I'm afraid there's no joke."

Julia's groan hurt Sam's eardrum. "How could you, darling? What on earth possessed you to get married?"

"I'm thirty-two years old," Sam countered. "Wouldn't you say it was about time?"

"You've lost your mind," Julia said, her voice rising in agitation. "I can't think of another reason for such a foolish, foolish act."

"Love?" Sam asked, enjoying her role as devil's advocate. "Isn't that why most people get married?"

Julia made a dismissive sound that neatly conveyed her basic distrust in the institution of marriage. "I know you too well, my darling. There's more to this than meets the eye."

"You're right about that," Sam said, wearying of her mother's outrage. "I'm pregnant." She waited for a reaction but when none was forthcoming she went on. "You're very quiet, Mother. Are you overwhelmed at the thought of becoming a grandmother?"

"Oh, God." Julia groaned loudly. "I wish you wouldn't say things like that."

"Wouldn't you say it's about time for that, too? I'm thirty-two, which makes you—"

"Old enough to know better than to discuss my age."

"So why did you call, Julia?" Sam found herself resenting this intrusion into her new life. "And how on earth did you get the number?" She couldn't remember the last time her mother had telephoned her. It had to be at least three years.

"I called to tell you I'm here for you if you decide you made a mistake."

Sam stared at the phone as if it had sprouted wings and a tail. The statement was so unlike Julia as to sound downright foreign. "I'm happily married, Mother. I haven't made a mistake."

"Duncan Stewart is a difficult man, darling."

"What did you say?"

Julia's sigh rippled through the wires. "Don't pretend you didn't hear what I said. Your husband is well-known as a difficult man. There's no crime in failure."

"I have no idea what you're talking about."

"Darling, everyone knows he's carrying a torch for his ex. He was devastated when Lana moved out, and most people think he'd take her back in an instant if she'd have him."

Two big fat tears of annoyance slid down Sam's cheeks. "I'd like to know why you felt compelled to share that with me, Mother."

"Well, isn't that obvious?" Julia asked. "I'm wor-

ried about you and I don't want you left with a broken heart.''

''My heart's in no danger,'' she declared, brushing away the tears with the back of her hand.

''I hope not,'' Julia said, ''because there's nothing worse than loving a man who doesn't love you.'' She paused. ''Especially if you're expecting his baby.''

Chapter Eleven

Duncan found Sam in the dining room an hour later. She was bent over a thick black Filofax, and the sound of her fountain pen scratching against the pages filled the air.

"Your mother is well?" he asked from the doorway.

She looked up and it seemed to take a second for her to recognize him. "Yes," she said. "My mother's well."

"Was she surprised to hear about the wedding?"

"You could say that." She scribbled another line then capped her pen. "We need to talk, Duncan."

He sat down across the table from her. It was clear the conversation with her mother had upset her. "I'm listening, lassie."

"My files will be arriving from the States tomorrow or the next day," she said, "and I need a place to set up an office."

"An office?" That was the last thing he'd expected to hear from her.

"Yes," she said, all business. "I'm still on salary with Wilde & Daughters. The sooner I get my office situation straightened out, the sooner I can earn my keep.''

"You're in a hurry," he observed, leaning back in his seat. "You've been here less than twenty-four hours."

An odd expression shadowed her eyes. "And another twenty-four wouldn't change a thing," she said. "The business has always been my top priority."

He felt her words like a knife in the heart. "And the baby?"

Her cheeks reddened. "The baby obviously comes before business."

"Aye," he said slowly, "that's what it says in our agreement."

"I don't need an agreement to put my baby first."

"What is it you need to establish an office?" he asked.

"I need quite a bit," she began. "Fax machine, telephone, a printer, file cabinets, a desk." She paused. "And a place to put them."

"You can put them anywhere you wish, lassie. The room is yours to choose."

"I saw a room overlooking the garden that would work quite well."

"Then it's yours." He would put no obstacles in her way as long as she understood the child came before all else.

She nodded. High color still stained her cheeks, from anger or embarrassment he couldn't say. "Now my next question is, where do I go to find office equipment?"

"There aren't many choices in Glenraven."

"That's what I was afraid of."

"I can take you into town and introduce you to Dixon the stationer."

"I'd appreciate it."

"I'll bring the car around."

WILLIAM DIXON was a garrulous old man with an encyclopedic knowledge of business equipment and suppliers. Within an hour he had helped Sam place orders for everything she needed and a few things she didn't.

"I'll see to it myself, Samantha," he said as she handed over her American Express card. "You'll be all set up by Friday."

"You've been a wonderful help, William," Sam said as she signed the receipt. "I don't know what I would've done without you."

"Glenraven is small but enterprising," he said, winking at Duncan, who stood near the doorway. "We even have a web site."

Sam laughed, but she noticed that Duncan only managed a quick smile. The charged atmosphere that had existed between them in his studio had been replaced by silence and unease, and she blamed her mother for the change.

If Julia had been looking to undermine Sam's self-confidence, she'd succeeded beyond her wildest dreams. Although maybe it was a good thing to be reminded this wasn't a love match, not by any stretch of the imagination. For a little while, in the privacy of his studio, she'd forgotten everything but how she felt beneath his gaze.

It was better this way, she thought, as she followed Duncan outside. With everything else in her life turned upside down, she needed the predictability of work. Work was something she understood. All those neat vertical lines of numbers eager to be organized into ever neater rows. Even when the numbers argued with you, you could find a logical reason for it if you knew where to look.

So far, life had turned out to be much less predictable.

"Are you hungry?" Duncan asked as they started down the street.

"A little," she admitted.

"We could go back to the castle—"

"That's fine," she said.

He looked at her, a half smile on his face. "You didn't let me finish, lassie. We could go back to the castle or stop at the Heather and the Thistle."

"The latter," she said, nodding. "That sounds wonderful."

He put his hand under her elbow and shepherded her up the narrow street and around the corner. The streets were quiet. Duncan nodded at two elderly women who whispered as they walked by, and he waved at a trio of men who stood talking in front of a place called Drummond's. People seemed to like Duncan but they gave him a wide berth, as if they recognized he wasn't quite one of them, even though his history was tightly woven with Glenraven's.

He pushed open the door to the Heather and the Thistle and motioned her inside. The pub was dark and a little smoky, but not unpleasantly so. It smelled faintly like Guinness but more so of bread baking in some back room. The place bore little resemblance to the noisy, brightly lit chain restaurants she knew back home, and she loved it all the more for that fact. She couldn't remember ever feeling so instantly, completely comfortable.

An attractive young woman with a mane of fiery red hair approached them. She smiled broadly at both Duncan and Sam.

"So William was telling the truth," she said, her eyes twinkling. "And here I called him a—" She laughed. "Well, I won't be telling you what I called him."

"This is Lucy," Duncan told Sam. "She grew up here at the Heather and the Thistle. Her parents own the place."

"Aye," said Lucy, nodding. "Single malt is mother's milk to me." Lucy wiped her right hand on her apron then extended it toward Sam. "And you're—"

"Samantha." She shook Lucy's hand. "Duncan's wife." *Duncan's wife.* That was the first time she'd actually said those words. How strange they'd sounded to her ears. *Duncan's second wife,* she could hear her mother say.

If Lucy found it strange, as Sam did, she didn't let on. "You're an American," Lucy said, not even trying to hide her curiosity. "How did he find you?"

"Actually I found him," Sam said. "I was looking for a pilot."

Lucy threw back her head and laughed. "And you hired our canny Scot as a pilot?"

"That's about the size of it," Sam said, aware of Duncan's interest in the conversation. "And he didn't tell me who he was."

"Oh, now I remember!" Lucy's face lit up.

"You're the one who was in the plane crash with Duncan."

"Yes," Sam said. "I'm the one."

"We were flooded with reporters after that," Lucy said, shaking her head, "but Glenraven proved so boring they finally went back to London."

"Aye," said Duncan. "We protect our own."

He and Lucy bantered back and forth and Sam found herself struck by the real affection between them. William Dixon had displayed the same warmth with Duncan, as had his clerks. God knew, Old Mag and Robby were devoted to him. What was there about her husband that inspired such loyalty?

"You're here to eat, not talk," Lucy said, glancing from Duncan to Sam. "The soup is good today, but the stew is better."

"Stew," said Duncan, "and a Guinness."

"Soup," said Sam, "and a glass of milk."

You could have heard a pin drop. It seemed to Sam that everyone in the crowded pub stopped talking and turned to stare at her.

"Milk," Lucy repeated, her eyes widening. "Can it be—"

"Aye," said Duncan, looking both proud and embarrassed. "It can."

Lucy let out a shriek of delight. "Duncan's having a baby!" she called, and next thing Sam knew, she was surrounded by happy, laughing strangers, all of whom had congratulations and good advice to offer her.

Duncan accepted the teasing with good-natured grace, but Sam couldn't help but notice the muscle twitching alongside his jaw. He'd never expressed anything but happiness over the baby—or at least, that's how she had perceived his reaction. Was it possible she'd misread the signals? When you came down to it, he was a stranger to her. She couldn't pretend to know how he felt about anything at all, except maybe the child she was carrying.

Now, looking at him as he fielded congratulations from his neighbors, she found herself wondering what he really thought about the changes in his life. Up until that moment she'd accepted everything he said at face value, not once questioning his feelings about becoming a father. Was he happy? Sad? Did he feel trapped by circumstances? Had he ever really thought about what the rest of his life would be like?

And, more to the point, had she?

SAMANTHA WAS QUIET on the way to the castle. She hadn't said much at all during lunch. They'd spent most of their time surrounded by well-wishers, and he'd seen the strain on her face by the time they said goodbye. The good citizens of Glenraven were an enthusiastic lot, but to his American bride, they must have sounded like jabbering monkeys. She'd get used to it one day but right now she looked exhausted.

"You didn't eat much," he observed as he negotiated one of a series of hairpin curves between town and home.

"I ate," she said.

"Is it the morning sickness?"

She chuckled softly. "At four in the afternoon?"

"Aye," he said, warmed by the sweet sound of her laughter. "That couldn't be the answer."

"Thank you for taking me into town," she said,

sounding very prim and formal. "William Dixon is a miracle worker."

"He will be if your purchases arrive on time."

"They will," she said. "I have confidence in him."

And in me, lassie? Do you have confidence in your husband?

In his studio that morning he'd felt the connection that had brought them together the first time. That sizzle of awareness that had sealed his fate. She'd been all softness and yielding curves, and it had taken all of his self-control to keep from taking her there in his studio.

They'd detailed how they would handle everything in their prenuptial agreement. Money. Work. Geography. But not how they would handle passion. No, they had an answer for every other problem life might throw their way—every one but that.

He parked the car around back and opened the door for Sam. She favored him with a quick impersonal smile and climbed from the car.

"I think I'm going to putter around the office," she said as they walked toward the kitchen door. "Try to figure out where I'll put things."

"You'll need help," he said.

"You should go back to your studio," she said. "That's what you should do. I'll worry about my office."

"How about this. I'll help you get the office ready then you can come back to the studio with me."

She hesitated just long enough for him to feel the fool. Was he that transparent then, his need for her shining through his simplest words? He raised his hand between them, as if the gesture could erase those words.

"An idea, lassie, and not a good one. My help doesn't come with strings attached."

Her expression softened and she placed a hand gently on his arm. "I never thought it did."

He followed her up the path to the kitchen door. Old Mag was stirring something at the stove when they stepped inside.

"Good thing you're back," she announced the second she saw Duncan. "If it's a telephone operator you want, then you best be hiring one." She pointed toward the kitchen table with her ladle. "Your messages."

The stack was almost an inch thick. Duncan picked them up and sifted through them. "These are for you," he said, handing a half dozen to Sam.

Her brow pleated. "For me?" She glanced at the messages and some of the furrows smoothed out. "Invitations!" she said, turning to Duncan. "This is amazing. How did they find out about me so fast?"

"Glenraven is a small place," he said. "And the people like to talk." He hadn't considered how it would feel to share her with other people. What they had together, what they'd created in that lawyer's office in Houston, seemed a thing apart from real life. Watching her as she talked with the customers at the Heather and the Thistle, he'd been reminded that there were facets to her personality he knew nothing about. He wouldn't have imagined his ambitious American businesswoman would seem so comfortable with the plainspoken, hardworking people of

Glenraven. Or that they would take her so quickly to their hearts.

"What about your messages?" she asked.

"The same. Everyone in town wants to meet you."

"It would take us all year to visit with everyone," she said.

"Aye, it would."

"And the more pregnant I get, the less likely I'll probably be to go visiting."

"There's that."

"So I think we should throw a party."

Behind them Old Mag's ladle clattered to the floor.

"A party," Duncan repeated. The last party the old castle had seen was at his wedding to Lana.

"It makes perfect sense," his new bride went on. "Throw open the doors and invite the entire town."

"Ach!" Old Mag muttered. "And more work for the innocent ones."

Duncan shot the housekeeper a sharp look, but Mag only glared at him more fiercely than before.

Sam turned to Mag. "I'm not afraid of hard work," she said, smiling at the old woman.

"I can afford extra help," Duncan said gruffly.

"So can I," Sam said, "but part of the fun of giving parties is the preparation."

Old Mag rolled her eyes. "'Tis the pregnancy speaking."

"You're right," Sam said, looking from Mag to Duncan. "It *is* the pregnancy speaking. My baby's going to grow up here, with all of these people around him. Why not start off on the right foot and show everyone a good time?"

To Duncan's surprise, Old Mag nodded her approval. He felt as though he was seeing his wife for the first time. He wished he'd thought of the party himself. The people of Glenraven were a close-knit group. They were loyal to their own and had little experience in welcoming newcomers into their midst. The best way to introduce Sam as one of their own was at an old-fashioned party, the kind the castle had been famous for in years gone by.

"When would you have this party?" he asked Sam.

Sam thought for a second. "In two weeks."

He looked at Old Mag. "How does that sound to you, old woman?"

"Two weeks, two months," Old Mag said, "too much work for a body either way."

"Two weeks," Duncan said.

"Two weeks!" Sam's face lit up with a smile. "This is going to be absolutely wonderful."

DUNCAN didn't come to bed that night.

Sam had bathed right after supper, then propped herself up in bed, surrounded by pillows, and set out making lists for work and the party. From the time she was a little girl, she'd loved to make lists. She listed her dolls, her daydreams, the places she wanted to visit and the things she hoped to do when she was grown up and on her own. She still loved making lists, but tonight she couldn't keep her mind on anything but Duncan.

From her window she could see the lights glowing inside his studio. She had no idea what his normal working schedule was. Was he a day person? A night owl? Did he work best in solitude or was a model a necessity for him? A ripple of excitement moved through her body as she remembered the thrilling intensity of being the focus of his undivided attention. He must have used models before to pose for him. Had they felt the same burst of pleasure as Sam had when he placed those big hands on her shoulders and moved her from position to position?

And what about his first wife? Julia had said Lana was beautiful, one of those actresses the camera adored. She must have posed for him. Probably many times. His work had always been almost unbearably erotic. His nudes had glowed with a sexual heat and passion that could only come from life. Duncan had loved his first wife, Julia had said. Loved her passionately until she walked out on him.

And what if he did? What business was it of Sam's if he'd loved the first Mrs. Stewart more than life itself? She was gone, and Sam was here. She and Duncan might not be the love match of the century, but they were legally married and expectant parents. Sam might not have first claim—or any claim at all—on his heart but she did have the first claim on his future. Or at least the baby did.

Suddenly the walls of the enormous bedroom seemed to be closing in on her. She climbed out of bed then slipped into her favorite Wedgwood blue silk robe and a pair of matching slippers. She hadn't been able to get the windows open, and the stagnant air made her feel a little queasy. Maybe if she stepped outside for a while and got some fresh air, she'd feel better.

She hurried from the room and made her way downstairs, trying to make as little noise as possible.

Not that it was so late. She just didn't want to bump into Old Mag and have to endure a round of the woman's questions.

She wouldn't have to ask you any questions, Sam. She'd know what you were up to the second she saw your face.

A fine mist hovered just above the lawn, giving the night a soft, almost ethereal glow. She felt like the heroine in a romance novel, gliding through the moonlit darkness in her silky robe, with her hair tumbling loose down her back. Of course, any good romance novel heroine deserved a hero. And, God knew, Duncan was certainly hero material. Not that that had anything to do with why she was outside, wandering across the damp grass toward the studio. She was simply getting some fresh air.

Once again the door to his studio was open. She hesitated for a second then knocked.

"Come in, lassie."

The sound of his voice in the dark made her shiver. *This is why you came out, Sam. Admit it.*

The studio lights were so bright that she had to shield her eyes with her hand against the glare.

"Sorry to disturb you," she said, as she waited for her eyes to adjust to the light. "I had a question about our party."

"It's after midnight," he observed. "You should be asleep."

"So should you."

He shook his head. "I work best at night."

"Do you?" The slightly flirtatious lilt to her voice surprised her. Her sisters were the flirts. Wasn't she supposed to be the serious one? She moved closer to his workbench. "Let me see."

His eyes narrowed and she felt the sharp edge of sexuality, the way she had the day they met. "As you wish, lassie."

Magic, she thought, staring at the unfinished sculpture. That was the only way to describe it. Again she found herself marveling at the way he'd somehow managed to transform cold marble into something warm and alive. The line of her throat and shoulders was more pronounced than before and she found herself touching her own throat in recognition.

"I've been having trouble with the spine," he said.

"Not so you'd notice." She gently rested her hand on the marble, amazed to be reminded that it was hard and cold to the touch. "This is so beautiful." She allowed her gaze to meet his. "You truly are gifted, Duncan."

His expression didn't betray his emotions at all, but Sam sensed a change in the atmosphere between them. Or at least she thought she did.

"Imagination can take me only so far, lassie. Would you pose for me again?"

A flutter happened deep in the pit of her stomach and she knew it was too soon to feel the baby move. What she was feeling had to do with her new husband. "I'm sure you could find a better model, Duncan."

"But she wouldn't be you."

His words galvanized her and she had to remind herself not to ascribe a deeper meaning to his statement. Not unless she wanted to complicate her life any more than it already was. "Now?" she asked him.

He nodded. "If you're not too tired."

"I'm not too tired." She couldn't remember the last time she'd felt so wide awake or ready for experience.

The chaise longue was still in the center of the room. She sat down primly, tucking her robe about her knees, and waited for some direction.

"The robe," he said, standing over her. "Could you—"

She undid the belt to her robe, willing her fingers to stop trembling. There was no reason to be nervous. She had her nightgown on beneath the robe. Besides, this had nothing to do with sex. At least, not for Duncan. This was about his work.

"I need to see the curve of your spine," he said as she folded the robe and draped it across the back of the chaise longue.

She nodded and lifted her hair off the back of her neck and let it fall across her chest.

"More than that, Samantha." His tone was neutral. Maybe too neutral. "I need the entire line."

She knew what he was asking. Slowly she lowered the right spaghetti strap on her nightgown, then the left one. The bodice fell away from her body, baring her torso to the waist. She felt more powerful in that moment than she'd ever felt in the boardroom. She crossed her arms over her breasts then leaned forward, elongating her spine in the way he'd told her to do.

The night air washed over her like a welcome caress. Maybe the gentle breeze would help dispel the heat gathering inside her chest.

Then again, maybe not.

He touched her shoulder to adjust her position and she felt as if he had set off a small fire beneath her skin. "Like this," he said, running his hand down the ridges of her spine. "Can you hold that?"

"Yes," she murmured. "Of course."

The position was awkward at best but she didn't care. Her back was to him yet she could sense when his eyes were skimming her body and when they weren't. Every now and then he would shift her slightly, the tiniest adjustment of angle and line, then return to his hammer and chisel. She could hear the tap, the soft crack of marble dropping away, the sound of his breathing.

She wondered if she would ever again hear the sound of his heart beating beneath her ear as he held her close.

And then she wondered if she'd lost her mind.

Chapter Twelve

Sam's files arrived the next day and her furniture the day after that, and she set about the job of arranging her office. Duncan helped her with the manual labor. He handled the desk and file cabinets as easily as she handled her laptop computer, and she found herself casting appreciative glances his way when she thought he wasn't looking. There was something overwhelming about a man in his prime and her husband certainly was that. She was almost disappointed when the furniture was in place and she got down to work.

They fell into a routine. Neither one talked about it but their life was acquiring a pattern as the days slid into each other. Her father had yet to return to Houston from his fishing trip but Sam was keeping up with work, thanks to her laptop and modem, her fax and couriers. She took long walks in the early afternoon. Sometimes she borrowed Duncan's car and drove into town on the pretext of needing toner for her copy machine or a certain kind of shampoo for her hair. The truth was, she loved Glenraven and the people she'd met there. They'd made her feel one of them from the very first day. Lucy at the Heather and the Thistle never failed to make her laugh with stories about Old Mag and Robby. William at the stationery store charmed her with his courtly manners. And there was Rose from the market and Gil from the flower shop and the people who stopped her on the street to let her know just how much they loved Duncan and how they prayed the two of them would be happy together forever and ever. He deserved to be happy, they said, lowering their voices, especially after "that other one."

There were times when she felt as if she'd stepped back through the centuries to the era when Duncan's castle was the center of that particular Scottish universe. He wasn't royalty. If he had a title, he'd never told her about it. But there was still something of nobility about him, and it was clear everyone else sensed it, too. She wondered what it was going to be like, raising a child in the middle of a history she didn't understand. She gathered up as many books of local history as she could find from Duncan's library and stacked them on the nightstand next to the bed.

One thing she knew was that there would be plenty of time to read.

Every night after dinner she walked to Duncan's studio, where she spent hours posing for him. He'd finished his first piece and was at work on a second, a frankly sensual study of her belly and hips. At first she'd resisted the pose, but her respect for his genius quickly overcame her natural reluctance and modesty, and she let her nightgown slither into a pool at her feet.

There was no disguising the roundness of her belly

anymore. She couldn't suck in her breath and make it flatten out. She was round and growing riper every day. Her breasts were large and swollen. She could easily trace the map of blue veins beneath the surface of her pale skin. Her waistline was quickly becoming a memory. The slender, lanky body she'd known for thirty-two years was gone and in its place was the curvy shape of a fertility goddess.

Which was exactly the earthy frankness Duncan seemed intent upon portraying.

They still hadn't decided exactly what he would do to fulfill his Wilde & Daughters Ltd. contract, but she wasn't too worried about it. There was plenty of time to decide on a piece and begin implementing the necessary work to begin mass production. At least that's what she told herself the rare times she even thought about that. She was so overwhelmed with the novelty of watching him at work, of being in some small measure his muse, that it was easy to let everything else slip away.

But the one thing she couldn't forget was the fact that he didn't share her bed. Not really. After a few hours of posing, he would walk her across the misty lawn to the castle. He would see her upstairs to their room. And then he would say good-night.

She'd stay awake for hours afterward, reading the history books or working on her myriad party lists, but what she was really doing was waiting for him. She knew he slept there. When she'd open her eyes in the morning, the imprint of his head on the pillow next to her was clearly visible. Did he lie there for a few minutes simply to allay any suspicions Old Mag might have? Did he sleep beside her, disappearing into his dreams? She had no idea. She hadn't been able to stay awake long enough to find out.

They said the first three months of pregnancy were about sleep and nausea, and she wouldn't dispute that statement. However, she was almost into her fourth month now and the deep lassitude of the first trimester still lingered. No matter how hard she tried, she never saw him climb into bed with her.

If Old Mag suspected anything, she never let on. Sam and the housekeeper worked a little every day on party preparations, and in doing so, began to forge a friendship of sorts. Oh, Old Mag was still watching out for Duncan's welfare with an eagle eye, but she made it clear that Sam was a pleasant surprise.

Even if she wasn't a Scotswoman.

Sam had decided she would do most of the cooking for the party. Old Mag would make some of her Scottish specialties, while Sam would turn her culinary skills toward recreating her favorite Texas recipes. She made two enormous pots of chili and tucked them into the freezer. She searched the Internet for the perfect recipe for barbecued beef and Southern fried chicken, sending her printer into overtime as it dashed out the recipes. Mag grumbled when Sam told her about the twenty pounds of potatoes they'd need for the potato salad, but Sam was insistent. "You'll love it," she told the housekeeper. "I promise you."

Of course, when it came to Old Mag, you couldn't be sure of anything. The housekeeper was filled with secrets. Sometimes Sam had the feeling that if she pushed the old woman just the slightest bit, those secrets would tumble out. She was tempted—what woman wouldn't want to know about her husband's life before she came along—but Sam had the strangest sense that she wouldn't like what she heard. Her mother's words kept coming back to her. *There's nothing worse than loving a man who doesn't love you...especially if you're expecting his baby.*

But she didn't love him, did she? They hadn't said one blessed thing about love when they hammered out their agreement at her lawyer's office. In fact, she thanked God every night that she didn't love Duncan Stewart, because if she did, she'd never be able to live the way they were living.

She didn't understand how she could feel the absence of something she'd never had, but there it was. There was an emptiness inside her that hadn't been there before. She'd always felt complete within herself, content to live her life alone with her work to keep her company. But it was all so different now. She longed for something she couldn't have, something she wasn't entirely certain existed. Something she couldn't define in words if her life depended on it.

She told herself it was the pregnancy, that women yearned for everything from pickles with ice cream to brand-new houses when they were carrying babies. The nesting instinct manifested itself in strange ways. Maybe the empty feeling inside her heart was nothing more than that.

DUNCAN WATCHED his wife with a kind of wonder as she moved through the days before the party. The differences between her old life in Houston and her new life at Glenraven were unfathomable, and yet she seemed to have settled in with more grace and enthusiasm than he would have imagined possible. Certainly more than he would have been able to manage were the situation reversed.

She worked for her family's company. She helped Old Mag with the party preparations, even though he'd insisted they hire help for the big day. She went into town on numerous errands and charmed everyone she met.

And she posed for him.

In the evening, long after supper was over, he'd hear a tap at the door to his studio. Then the door would swing open and she'd step inside, into the shimmering light, and he felt as if she'd brought the moon and the stars with her. They'd exchange a few words and then she would drop her robe into a pale blue puddle at her feet and stand there naked before him. More beautiful, more radiant than anything he'd ever seen.

He would position her on the chaise longue, his hands lingering on the outward flare of her hips, the glorious swell of her breasts. One time, two nights ago, their eyes met and he saw recognition in hers, the sense that she knew what he was feeling and that she might be feeling the same thing herself. He cursed himself for letting the moment pass. She would have been his if he'd asked.

He'd never been an indecisive man. He knew what he wanted and he took the shortest route to obtain it. But since Samantha came into his life, it seemed as if he moved two steps back for every one that brought him closer to her. They moved through their days on parallel tracks, and he wondered if he would ever find the way to bring those tracks together.

The party was set for Saturday evening. On Friday morning Samantha was scheduled for her first appointment with the gynecologist Lucy had recommended to her.

"You don't have to come along," his wife said to him as she fixed her hair in front of the bedroom mirror. Long strands of pale gold shimmered over her shoulders and down her back, and he frowned as she gathered it into sections and began to braid it close to her head. "You don't like French braids?" she asked his reflection.

"Nothing wrong with braids," he said. "But not for you."

Her hands worked swiftly, crossing and recrossing the sections into an intricate weave. "This is neat and functional, Duncan. Businesslike."

"That's why it's not right for you." A calculated risk, that statement. He'd jumped the track.

She said nothing. Her fingers continued braiding.

"I'll bring the car around," he said as she finished up.

She nodded. "I'll be right down."

Thirty minutes later they were ushered into the doctor's office. They called Duncan into the examination room once Sam was in position on the table. He waited while the doctor attached sensors to her belly then began the ultrasound process.

Duncan and Samantha watched the flickering images on the monitor then looked at each other. Neither one could make sense out of the amorphous shapes and shadows, and they waited quietly for the doctor to identify what they were seeing.

"Over here," said the doctor, pointing to the lower right portion of the screen. "See? Those are the feet."

Duncan narrowed his eyes and leaned closer to the monitor and suddenly, miraculously, the image rose up before him and everything else snapped into place.

Next to him he heard a small cry from his wife, a sharp note of joy he would remember for the rest of his life. He reached for her hand and she clasped it tightly.

"Oh, Duncan—" Her voice caught and she stopped.

He bent and pressed a kiss to her forehead, imprinting the warmth of her skin, her sweet scent, to memory. Few moments in life presented themselves with such singular clarity, such life-changing certainty. A man's first glimpse of his child was one of them.

THEY LEFT the doctor's office an hour later and drove deeper into the Highlands. They didn't talk about it but Duncan knew he'd made the right decision when he saw the way Samantha settled deeper into her seat and smiled.

He loved this wild and rugged land with his whole being and he wanted her to love it, too. If she couldn't love him, if that wasn't in their future, then maybe his beloved Scotland could work its magic and draw her closer.

Bailey Park was to the west, facing the sea. He parked near an outcropping of rock then went around to open her door for her. There was a peacefulness to her expression that he'd never seen before, and she gave him her hand as if she'd been doing so every day of their lives.

In a way he could no longer remember those days before he met her. A man would be wise to remember the darkness even in the face of radiant light, but it was already too late. She was in his blood now, even if she never knew it.

THEY SAT TOGETHER on the cliff and watched the angry waters slam against the rocks below. Duncan kept his arm around her, and Sam found herself leaning against him. It wasn't a conscious choice. Her body simply moved toward him as if doing so was the most natural thing on earth.

Every now and again she'd glance in his direction and invariably he was looking at her, those beautiful eyes of his filled with so much emotion that she had to look away.

It's not for you, Sam, and don't go thinking it is. It was for the baby. The child they'd made together.

The baby was real to her in a way it hadn't been until that moment in the doctor's office with the gel and the sensors and that gauzy, miraculous picture that now rested in the back seat of Duncan's car. She wondered if he felt the same way. The baby they'd talked about in Houston and married for in Las Vegas and come to Scotland to raise—that baby was a living, breathing human being who sucked its thumb and changed position with the restless grace of a dancer on a very small stage.

She felt overwhelmed by the wonder of it all and she was certain that Duncan shared her feelings. They didn't talk or banter or analyze. They didn't need to. It was all between them as they sat close together and imagined life thundering like the sea.

THEY RETURNED to the castle in time for lunch. Duncan and Sam ate quickly then went their separate ways. He went to the studio while Sam busied herself in the kitchen making the potato salad while Old Mag followed the hired cleaning help from room to room, pointing out their shortcomings. Sam ladled the potato salad into a huge earthenware bowl, covered it securely with plastic wrap, then somehow managed to find a place for it in the packed refrigerator.

From there she went to her office where the mountain of paperwork seemed to have grown while she was away. She checked for messages. Still nothing from Lucky or her sisters. Not that she expected to hear from them yet. Lucky wasn't due back from his vacation for another two weeks, about the same time Martie and Trask would come home from their vacation. And as for Frankie—well, Sam wouldn't hazard a guess. Her flighty little sister could pop up anywhere at anytime. The world's rules had little to do with the way Frankie lived her life. Or at least that was how it had always seemed to Sam.

She wasn't sure exactly why she'd asked her mother to join them at the party but she had. Of course, Julia had written immediately, saying she didn't know if she could fit the party into her busy London social life. She'd just have to see. Motherhood had never been Julia's strong suit, and, until recently, Sam hadn't spent much of her emotional energy wishing things had been different. Her pregnancy, however, had lowered her emotional defenses and she found herself thinking about her mother more often than she had in the thirty-two years that went before.

Wishful thinking, that's what it was. Wishful thinking that had absolutely nothing to do with reality.

They'd decided to bypass a hot dinner tonight. It seemed to Sam they all had enough to do without worrying about that. She wandered into the kitchen around eight o'clock and fixed herself a sandwich and milk. There was no sign of Duncan anywhere. Even his studio was dark. Not that she would have had time to pose for him tonight. She needed to bathe and condition her hair and draw up a last-minute list of all the other things that needed doing before the party began tomorrow.

She washed her plate and glass, dried them, then put them away in the cupboard. Satisfied that the kitchen looked orderly and clean enough for Old Mag, she went upstairs.

DUNCAN LANDED his new Cessna at the strip outside Glenraven a little past ten o'clock. Summer days in the Highlands were long and beautiful and the sky still held more than a memory of light. He'd spent the late afternoon and evening in Glasgow, searching for the perfect wedding ring for Samantha. He'd finally found it, a beautiful circle of silver and gold, and he'd waited while the jeweler painstakingly inscribed it with Sam's initials and Duncan's and the date of their wedding. It was a sentimental gesture and he knew it. A gesture that came with an element of risk attached to it, but for Duncan, it was time.

She needed to know it was about more than the baby. That wasn't what had drawn him across the Atlantic in search of her. She called to him, his bride did, to the deepest and most forgotten part of his heart.

He would give it to her tomorrow night after the party. After the guests left and the music faded away.

When it was only the two of them and the future stretching before them. A future he'd stopped believing was possible until she came into his life.

SAM TOOK a long warm shower. She took her time afterward, enjoying those wonderful heated bath towels, the slippery feel of her body lotion, the delicious slither of her nightgown as it slid over her shoulders and breasts. She'd never considered herself a particularly sensual person but lately she seemed to be almost unbearably aware of her body, of how it moved and felt. Things she'd never thought of before, like the coolness of the sheets as she climbed into bed and settled in. Her belly felt heavier than before. When she lay on her side, she could feel the shifting weight within her.

Her baby, she thought. Their child. It all seemed so much more real to her than it had when she woke up that morning. She'd pinned the sonogram picture to the bulletin board behind her desk, but she really didn't need to look at it anymore. She had every shape and shadow memorized, from the tiny feet to the little thumb already firmly in his or her mouth. The doctor had been unable to determine the baby's sex, but Sam found it honestly didn't matter either way. She finally understood the expectant parents' prayer. "Just let the baby be healthy. That's all we ask."

A breeze fluttered the window curtains, and she

caught the scent of heather mingled with lavender and mint and all the other fragrant herbs in Mag's garden. The combined smells were so heady and evocative that she almost felt dizzy from them. She placed her hand against the swell of her stomach and closed her eyes. The bed was soft and welcoming. The night air was magnificent. Her baby was growing stronger with every day that passed. Tomorrow they'd open their home to the townspeople and her life as one of them would be finally launched.

If only it were that easy to launch a marriage.

DUNCAN HID THE RING in his studio, tucking it behind a piece of marble he had earmarked for his next study of Samantha. He liked the heft of the ring. The warm gold and cool silver would wrap themselves around her finger, reminding her of the commitment they'd made to each other. Of the life they'd pledged to share.

At least, that was his hope as he walked up the pathway to the castle.

Old Mag and Robby were sitting at the table as he entered the kitchen.

Mag sent him a look. "It's about time you be coming home."

"He doesn't have to answer to you, old woman," Robby said. "Only I have that privilege."

Duncan grabbed a piece of shortbread from the plate in the center of the table. They spent a few moments talking about tomorrow's party then he asked, "Where's Samantha?"

"Don't ask me," Mag said. "I will not spy on your bride."

"He didn't ask you to spy on her," Robby said, his voice rising in exasperation. "All he asked is—"

"Don't worry about it," Duncan said, starting to laugh. "I'll find her."

She wasn't in her office. He checked the library, figuring she might be watching the television, but she wasn't there either. Disappointment washed over him. He'd hoped to find her still awake.

He started up the stairs to the bedroom. He wondered if she had any idea how much he looked forward to the hours they spent together in his studio each night. The way her mind leaped from subject to subject. The powerful beauty of her face. The lush glory of her body. The whole splendid package.

The lights were off in their room, same as every night. He went into the bathroom, showered, then, naked, opened the bathroom door to find the lights on in the bedroom and his wife sitting, propped up against the headboard, looking straight at him. There was nothing coy about her look. Her gaze moved over his body slowly, deliberately, moving from his face to his chest, from his belly to his legs.

"We're back where we started," she said finally, her voice a little husky. A lot enticing.

The last thing he wanted to do was misinterpret her meaning.

He walked toward the bed the same way he walked toward it every night when she was asleep, her body curled away from his, lost somewhere in her dreams.

"I'm sorry I woke you up," he said, throwing back the covers.

"You didn't wake me up," she said. "I heard your car in the driveway."

"I went to Glasgow for the afternoon," he said, climbing into the bed beside her.

"Business?" she asked, her tone light and casual.

"Partly." He met her eyes. "Will you be leaving the light on, lassie?"

She looked away briefly then back again. "Do you want me to?"

There was no denying the invitation. He leaned toward her, aware of the sweet scent of her body. She didn't move. Her gaze held his steadily. Completely.

"Are you sure?"

Her eyelids fluttered shut for a second. "I'm sure."

She was in his arms in a heartbeat. He pushed aside the straps of her silky nightgown and pressed his mouth against the warm curve of her shoulder as fierce emotion swelled inside his heart. He heard her soft cry and then felt the gentle touch of her hand as she stroked his hair with the softest fingers. She smelled like soap and rain and woman and he eased the gown from her body, kissing his way downward. He worshiped her belly, its fertile roundness, worshiped it with the palms of his hands, his fingertips, his mouth.

She was so soft, so delicately made that he felt himself holding back, not wanting to overwhelm her with the intensity of all that she made him feel. He kissed his way over her belly's swell until he felt the brush of her soft tangle of golden curls against his mouth.

She moaned softly. He hesitated, but she moved against him in a way that told him everything he needed to know.

ALL SAM KNEW was that she never wanted this to end. She was pure sensation. Her skin was alive with it. She registered his presence in every cell and fiber of her being. His smell, his heat, his power—all of it. Everywhere.

And it wasn't close to being enough.

She wanted to feel him inside her, deep inside. She wanted it more than she wanted to draw her next breath. She could feel her defenses shattering, hear the sound of her heart as it cracked open, and there was nothing she could do but let it happen. All she wanted to do—all she could do—was reach out to him, snake her hands along his shoulders and back, let the heat from his body burn her palms. His muscles rippled where she touched and her power over him only made her want him more.

He was so beautiful to her, so wonderfully male, that she couldn't find her voice. She felt herself opening to him, shameless in her desire to be touched and caressed, to feel the wet warmth of his mouth and tongue against all her secret places. He did magical things to her, sent her spiraling to heaven and back again in the blink of an eye, in an eternity.

And then suddenly it wasn't enough. She yearned for him in body and soul. She wanted to be overpowered by him, covered by his welcome weight and warmth, filled by him.

A second later he moved his way up her willing body, kissing, stroking, worshiping, until their mouths were only a kiss away. He touched her lower lip with the tip of his tongue and a shudder of intense pleasure rippled through her. She could taste her essence on him, sweet and salty, forbidden yet somehow familiar.

His body was big and strong and warm, and in the room's silence she thought she could hear the sounds of their hearts beating. He started to say something but she pressed her fingertip to his lips.

"Don't talk," she whispered. "Not now."

Talking would destroy the magic and she wanted very much to believe in magic. If she didn't, she might remember all the reasons this wasn't right. Why she had no business being here in this strange country, with this man she barely knew. How she wished it could be so much more than it was.

HIS BRIDE'S BODY trembled. Duncan could feel the restless energy building inside her as he touched the slope of her breast with a gentle hand. Such powerful beauty. He wanted to worship her the way the pagans had worshiped the earth in all her richness and fertility. He wished he had the ring with him now, to tell her finally all that she meant to him. Had meant to him from the first moment he looked into her eyes.

But he was too far drawn into passion's heart to stop now. There would be time tomorrow for what needed to be said. Tonight was for pleasure.

Warm skin to warm skin. Heart to heart. The power of touch shocked them both to their marrow and for an endless time all they did was look into each other's eyes.

He had never done this before, really looked at a woman the way he was looking at her. Before, he always saw the topography, the play of light and shadow, the swell of muscle and architecture of bone. He saw all of that in her and so much more. He saw straight through to her heart.

And no one had ever made Sam feel the way he did. Shy and bold. Terrified and safe. Wanting it all now, everything, in every way possible. She was greedy for him, hungry to gather him into her, and so she moved beneath him, her hips rising and falling, rising and falling, until he understood all that she'd been trying to say.

He positioned himself between her thighs, caressing her lightly with his hand, making sure she was ready for him. He was all coiled muscle and heat, and it would take very little to push him over the brink.

She made a small sound then, a low moan deep in the back of her throat, as she drew him into her body. A primitive sense of possession, of fierce, blood-hot victory, swept over him and he began to move, slowly at first then faster, waiting each time for her to pick up the tempo before he changed it again.

And she did.

Every time. In every variation.

They moved as if they'd been together since the dawn of time, the kind of seamless erotic lovemaking that inspired poetry, and when it was over they lay there together for a very long time, as the silence around them grew more charged.

She wanted to say something but couldn't find her voice.

He wanted to tell her but couldn't find the words.

In deep and plangent silence, they fell asleep.

Chapter Thirteen

Sam's mother called at eight the following morning to convey her regrets that she wouldn't be at the party that afternoon.

Sam, who had been in the middle of drying her hair, found it difficult to hide her annoyance. "Mother, we've both known you weren't coming from the day I sent you the invitation. Why did you wait until the last minute to tell me?"

"I don't like your attitude one bit, Samantha. I'd hoped I would be able to rearrange my schedule and join you but I'm afraid that won't be possible. I wanted to meet this man you've found yourself married to."

Sam sat on the edge of the bed and switched the phone to her other ear. "Is everything okay, Mother?" she asked politely.

Julia was silent.

"Mother?" Sam raised her voice. "Is everything okay?" she repeated. She and Julia weren't close but she did love her mother despite everything.

"Darling, I didn't want to go into this," Julia said.

"Mother, if there's something, please—"

"I had an eye job two weeks ago," Julia said. "I'm still bruised."

Sam stared at the phone the way people on television sitcoms liked to do. "You had an eye job?"

Julia's laugh was amused. "Darling, this isn't my first. Just the first one you've heard about."

By the time Sam hung up the phone, she had learned more than she'd ever wanted to know about eye jobs, face-lifts and liposuction. To think she'd always thought her mother's stunning good looks were the result of great genes and good nutrition.

She felt vaguely depressed as she went into the bathroom to finish drying her hair. Truth was, she'd been depressed ever since she woke up that morning to find Duncan long gone. His pillow was smooth. The covers had been pulled into place. For a second she'd wondered if she'd dreamed the entire wonderful interlude of the night before, but there was no denying the gentle ache between her thighs, the well-used feel of her body.

She finished arranging her hair in a sleek braid then walked into the bedroom to dress for the party. She wasn't entirely certain what you were supposed to wear to a summer party in the Highlands but figured she couldn't go too far wrong with a sundress in a buttery shade of yellow. Besides, it was one of the few things that still fit her comfortably and left enough room for her to breathe. Next week she would have to ask Duncan if he would take her to Glasgow or Edinburgh so she could shop for some new clothes to see her through the rest of her pregnancy.

Her dress was draped over the bed, its soft yellow folds drifting gracefully across the pure white sheets.

A wave of heat flared deep inside her body as she remembered the passion they'd shared less than twelve hours ago.

If it was that good, then where is he?

She hated when that nasty little voice of reason popped up with one of those unanswerable questions. She had been terribly disappointed to wake up and find him gone and his side of the bed already cold.

There's a difference between sex and love, Sam. You're old enough to know that.

Or was she? The line had blurred for her last night, making her feel more vulnerable than she ever had in her life. She was glad the party was today. With a crowd around and lots of music and dancing, there wouldn't be time to think. She reached for her sundress and slipped it over her head.

"Lassie?"

She spun around, the dress sliding down her body, and saw Duncan standing in the doorway. For a second she thought she was dreaming or that somehow, some way, she'd managed to step through some portal in time to the days of warriors and lairds. If she'd ever harbored the notion that there was anything remotely humorous or effeminate about a man in a kilt, the sight of her husband in Stewart plaid put that idea to rest.

He was, in a word, magnificent.

"Duncan!" she said, letting her surprise mask the wild rush of desire. "I didn't hear you come in."

"I didn't mean to frighten you."

"You didn't frighten me," she said, struggling with the zipper of her sundress. "You surprised me, that's all."

He motioned for her to come closer to him. She didn't move.

"Come here, lassie," he said, his voice a rough caress. "I'll zip your dress."

She'd spent many years zipping up her own dresses but still she went to him like a docile child. "Have you been up a long time?" she asked as she felt his hands against her spine.

"Since before dawn." His fingers brushed lightly against her skin and her breath caught. "Lift your hair. I don't want to catch it in the zipper."

She reached back and lifted the braid. The metallic rasp of the zipper sounded very loud to her ears. "There's a little hook at the top," she said.

"Aye. It's done."

She let the braid fall between her shoulder blades and stepped away from him, feeling terribly disappointed. If last night had meant anything at all to him, you wouldn't know it by his manner. "How's everything going?" she asked. "Are the tables set up?"

"The staff is very efficient," he said. "Robby supervised the outdoor crew and they had everything ready an hour ago."

"I'm sure Mag is keeping a close eye on the kitchen help."

"You'll have to find out for yourself, Samantha. No man would dare invade her territory today."

Sam laughed. "She is protective of her kitchen, isn't she?"

"Aye. I couldn't believe she allowed you to use it."

"Mag and I have reached an accommodation."

"She likes you."

"I wouldn't go that far," Sam said, pleased despite herself.

"I saw her sampling your potato salad."

"You're joking!"

"Ask her," he said.

"I will."

Sam loved the banter but she had the sense that he was using it to avoid what they'd shared the night before. Which told Sam much more than she wanted to know about the real state of their marriage.

Better to know where you stand, Sam. That way you won't get hurt.

She could enjoy making love with him, raising their child together.

But if she was looking for a real marriage, the kind that was based on love—well, that was the one thing she'd never have.

THERE WAS SO MUCH Duncan wanted to say to his bride, but it would have to wait until after the party. Their neighbors had begun to arrive an hour ago and Robby said they'd been asking for the newlyweds. Tonight would be time enough for him to show her how he felt. How he'd always felt.

Tonight after the dancing and the music, after they'd claimed their place as a couple in front of all of Glenraven. Tonight would be time enough.

"Does this dress look okay?" his beautiful wife asked as she stood before him. She had changed from the yellow dress to a blue one then back again to the yellow.

"You're a bonny lass," he said, knowing how far short of reality his meager words fell.

"The dress," she said again, placing her hands on her belly. "Maybe I should change into something else."

"It's perfect," he said. *As perfect as you are.* "Our guests are waiting for us, Samantha."

She took another long look at herself in the mirror then shuddered. "This is terrible."

"You'll outshine the sun."

She met his eyes and started to laugh. "You'll say anything to keep me from changing my clothes again, won't you?"

"Aye," he said. "I will."

"All right," she said, smoothing the skirt of her soft yellow dress, "let it be on your head when your friends whisper about your poor choice in wives."

She said it lightly but he thought he caught the slightest hint of real insecurity. It baffled him. How could she look in the mirror and see less than the goddess he saw?

They went downstairs and through the kitchen. The yard out back had been set up with tables and chairs, tents, grills, all manner of things necessary for party giving.

"It looks like the entire town is out there," Sam said.

"You invited them," he reminded her. "This was your idea."

"Tell me again why I thought it was such a good one," Sam said as they approached the door.

"Don't be nervous. Half the town already knows and loves you. Once the other half meets you, they'll love you, too."

She cupped the swell of her belly with her hands

and he knew what she was thinking. *This is for the baby*.

And it was. He wouldn't deny that. But it was also about the two of them. She would know that tonight when he gave her the ring.

SAM'S NERVOUSNESS vanished the second they stepped outside. The warmth of their welcome far surpassed the late July sunshine as they were greeted by their happy, laughing neighbors. Sam was swept off in a crowd of women and girls, all of whom wanted to know everything there was to know about her marriage to Duncan and the baby they were expecting.

In her old life back in Houston, Sam would have been looking for the nearest escape hatch. Business situations were easy for her. Social situations were anything but. Yet there she was, surrounded by scores of people she barely knew, and she felt happier and more at ease than she had in years. The good women of Glenraven showered her with advice about her baby. Everything from morning sickness to false labor to teething—they covered it all. Sam's head was spinning with information, and she was thankful when the lawn games began and they all rushed off to play. She took the opportunity to slip into the house for a moment's rest and a tall glass of very cold water.

Duncan followed her into the kitchen. "Is something wrong?"

"Just thirsty," she said. "Shouldn't you be out there, running around with everybody?"

"A man needs his own cheering section for inspiration."

She took a long sip of water. "Cheering is about as much as I can do."

"And it's all I'll ask for now."

What a strange remark. She looked at him carefully. The same face, the same glorious features. But something was different. Some essential ingredient had changed, and she couldn't quite put her finger on what it was.

SAM'S POTATO SALAD turned out to be an enormous success with her Glenraven neighbors.

"Have you any more of this?" asked Gordon Thornton, the local banker. "I've never tasted its like."

"I'd love the recipe, Samantha," said Elizabeth Macfadden, wife of the town eccentric. "I'd serve it at the next church gathering."

Sam, whose culinary skills were extremely limited, preened over the compliments.

"You were right, lassie," Old Mag said as the two of them went inside to fill more serving bowls. "Your American salad is disappearing."

Sam almost passed out cold on the kitchen floor. Old Mag had admitted she was human, after all. "It's one of the few things I can cook, Mag. I was praying it would go over well."

"And your chili," Mag went on, shaking her head. "I think they starved themselves for a week before comin' here, the way they swarmed about the tables."

Sam laughed as she took the rest of the potato salad out of the refrigerator. "They have been eating a lot, haven't they?" She met Mag's eyes. "Seems to me they made quick work of your contributions, too.

Your sausages disappeared the second we put them on the table.''

"Ach," Mag mumbled, obviously pleased by Sam's compliment. "They fear my evil tongue if they don't eat my food."

The two women worked well together. The weeks of party planning had somehow bonded them, and Sam was delighted with the outcome. Mag and Robby were Duncan's surrogate parents. They fussed over him, chided him and occasionally even ordered him around, and now they were doing that to Sam, as well. She had the feeling there was no greater acceptance.

"We still haven't heard all the details about your wedding," William Dixon's wife, Sally, said as they all dug into their plates of cake and ice cream.

Sam met Duncan's eyes. "There isn't that much to tell," she said, wondering how she was going to manage to sidestep the truth.

"Love at first sight," Duncan said.

Sam's breath caught in her throat. He said it so easily, so naturally, that if she didn't know better she might believe him. "We—well, we didn't know each other very long when we, um, when we decided to get married." Every word she said was true, but it sounded as if she was piecing it together from whole cloth.

"Samantha thought our Duncan was a pilot," William Dixon said to everyone's amusement. "She hired him to fly her someplace and they had that crash alongside the loch."

"You still owe me, lassie," Duncan said, putting his arm around her shoulders. "A deal's a deal."

They all laughed except for Sam. That's what their

marriage was, wasn't it? A deal between two strangers who just happened to be expecting a baby together.

She patted her stomach. "Don't worry," she said in what she hoped was a lighthearted tone. "I think you'll like the compensation."

That got another roar of laughter from their friends.

"I wish you'd waited to marry here in Glenraven," one of the women said. "It's been a long time since we saw a beautiful wedding in the chapel."

"You should have let us be part of it," said another woman. "I can't believe you'd deny us the pleasure."

Duncan handled it better than she ever could. "That's why we're having this party, Annie. This is our celebration."

"And we'll have an even bigger party for the baby's christening," Sam promised. "The biggest you've ever seen."

"No more talking," Robby called out. "Time for the dancing to begin."

As if on cue, she heard the skirl of bagpipes, followed by the sight of five kilted pipers marching over the hill. Down through the centuries, how many other Stewart wives had stood where she was standing and seen the same thrilling sight? She felt connected to each and every one of them.

"Let's dance Strip the Willow," Lucy from the Heather and the Thistle suggested.

"No," said Duncan, his arm still draped around Sam's shoulders. "An eightsome reel."

Lucy looked disappointed but she nodded.

"Why the eightsome reel over Strip the Willow?" Sam asked him.

"Because you're pregnant, lassie. Strip the Willow downs the strongest of us."

There was little she could say to that. She hadn't a clue what any of the dances entailed.

"I'm not much of a dancer," she admitted as the music swelled around them.

"You'll learn soon enough."

"Don't bet on it."

"Americans square-dance, don't they?"

"Not every American," she said, laughing. "But most Texans do."

"Then you'll have no trouble."

"We'll see about that," she murmured. At least they called square dances. Here in Scotland you were expected to actually know what you were doing.

To Sam it seemed like a cross between a line dance and a square dance, but the effect was one hundred percent Scottish. Men in kilts spun past her, in tartans of red and green and black. One young father held his baby daughter to his shoulder as he danced, imprinting the traditions of a proud nation in her memory. This time next year the proud father would be Duncan.

The eightsome reel was easy to grasp, and before Sam knew it, she'd relaxed enough to actually enjoy herself.

She had Duncan to thank for that. Every time they came together she had the sense she was flying, as if her feet had somehow left the ground and she was suspended by happiness alone.

"We should do this every week," she said to him as they spun in tune to the lively music. "Make it a tradition."

His smile was wider and more open than she'd ever seen it. "And what about when you're seven months along? What then?"

"Then I'll watch everyone else dance," she said, laughing with the sheer delight of music and movement.

"You're having a good time?"

"A wonderful time. In fact, if I—" She stopped as she realized he wasn't listening to her. He was looking over her right shoulder in the direction of the path that curved up the hill to the castle. So were Old Mag and Robby and at least a dozen other people. "Duncan," she said. "Is something wrong?"

He didn't answer. She turned in time to see a small, curvy woman climb from a black car. The woman wore a pale blue suit that hugged her tiny waist and round hips. She walked toward them with the kind of feline grace that always made Sam feel big and clumsy. This time was no exception.

"Do you know her?" she asked. "Who is she?"

But he wasn't listening to her. He dropped his arm from her shoulders and moved toward the woman in the blue suit.

"Duncan!" Sam started after him but Old Mag pulled her back.

"Don't follow him," the housekeeper said. "He will take care of the likes of her."

A terrible sense of foreboding filled Sam's chest. "Who is she, Mag?" she asked quietly, certain of the answer.

"Ach, lassie." Tears filled Old Mag's faded blue eyes. "That's the one who broke his heart."

"DARLING!" Lana walked toward Duncan with her arms outstretched. "It's been *so* long."

Duncan stopped short. He had no need of her touch. "Lana," he said, aware of the curious glances all around him. "Why are you here?"

"Such a greeting." Lana's gaze swept the crowd, obviously seeking an adoring fan upon whom to hang her hopes. "I expected a much warmer hello than that."

He refused to be pulled into that old and dangerous game. "Then you must be disappointed," he said mildly. Not one of the party guests had made a move to say hello to his ex-wife.

She dissembled prettily, acting as if he'd greeted her with a kiss. "A party, is it?" she asked, tilting her dark head in the direction of the music.

He turned away from Lana and toward Sam, who was watching him with serious blue eyes. She stepped forward and took her place by his side.

"Duncan?" Lana asked, unable to mask the sharp note of curiosity in her voice. "What's the occasion?"

Duncan took Sam's hand in his. "Our wedding," he said.

The color seemed to drain from Lana's face, and he was not above feeling a certain satisfaction.

"Oh, dear," Lana said, as her eyes slid over Sam then moved back to Duncan. "This certainly does complicate matters."

Duncan felt an uneasy pinch deep inside his gut. "We'll talk inside," he said, pitching his voice low so only Sam and Lana could make out his words.

"I'm not alone," Lana said. "Bryce is in the car."

Duncan felt his jaw harden into concrete. "And Bryce is—"

Lana's face glowed with studied brightness. "My love!" she said, opening her arms wide. "The man of my dreams."

Duncan refrained from pointing out that she had felt that way about at least three other men, himself included. It didn't matter to him whether or not she'd found the man of her dreams. All that mattered was getting this over with as soon as possible.

Lana motioned toward the car and a tall, lanky man with ginger-colored hair unfolded himself from the passenger seat and climbed out. He seemed all arms and legs as he ambled toward them.

"Do you have the car keys, darling?" she asked, all sweetness and concern.

The man shook his head. "I left them on the seat."

"Well, no matter," Lana said. But Duncan knew her well enough to see the signs of irritation that would later erupt into anger. She tossed her head, sending her dark hair drifting away from her face, then linked arms with the man next to her. "This is Bryce Stephenson."

Duncan extended his right hand. "Duncan Stewart."

"A pleasure." Bryce clasped Duncan's hand and the two of them stood there for a moment, locked in some kind of macho combat.

Duncan finally put an end to the stupidity. If he thought Duncan envied the man his future with Lana, then Stephenson was sorely mistaken. The only thing Duncan felt for the man was pity. He draped an arm around Sam's shoulders. "This is my wife, Samantha."

Stephenson's long jaw opened then closed quickly like a marionette's. He looked at Lana, who was observing all of them with spiderlike interest. "His wife?" he asked.

Lana placed a slender hand on the forearm of her latest victim. "We'll talk about it inside."

"Duncan." Samantha's voice was high and tight, not her usual low, sweet drawl. "We have guests who would love to get back to that eightsome reel."

Lana's eyebrows arched at the sound of Samantha's voice. "An American?" she asked, meeting Duncan's eyes. "How interesting."

The look he gave her stopped any further comment on her part.

He broke away from their group and called for attention. "Where's the music?" he bellowed. "I'd say it was time to Strip the Willow, wouldn't you?"

He motioned for the pipers to launch into their next song, and moments later the lawn was filled with happy, wildly dancing men and women.

He turned to Samantha, Lana and the ginger-haired man. "The library," he said, then took his bride's arm and headed inside.

FOR A SECOND, Sam considered pulling away from her husband and running as far and fast as she possibly could, but reason got the better of her. Whatever this was, the odds were she couldn't outrun it, no matter how hard she tried.

Anger rolled off Duncan in waves. Stephenson's confusion was almost palpable. Only Lana seemed in control of the situation. A fact that terrified Sam. What on earth could she possibly want with Duncan at this late date? It was obvious she wasn't looking for a reconciliation. Not if you could judge by the golfball-size diamond on her left ring finger. Still, the look of shock on both her face and Stephenson's when they heard about Duncan's marriage was unmistakable. Why would they care?

She felt almost dizzy with apprehension by the time they all found seats in the library.

Duncan was the first to speak. "What do you want, Lana?"

His ex-wife neatly crossed her left leg over her right then leaned forward. It wasn't hard to see why she was a movie star in Europe. She had that exotic, almost catlike allure that would translate beautifully on screen. Tiny, perfectly sculpted features, small bones, enormous brown eyes that dominated her face. A searing image of Lana's perfect little body moving sensuously atop Duncan's caused Sam to look away so no one noticed the angry red flush staining her face.

"This is a difficult topic to pursue, Duncan," Lana said, her gaze resting on Sam.

"Pursue it," Duncan said. He wasn't even pretending to play the gracious host. "We're having a party, Lana. We'd like to return to it."

Sam stood up, smoothing the skirt of her sundress. "Why don't I go out and make sure everyone's having a good time?" she offered.

Lana smiled at her. "That's a wonderful idea, dear."

"Sit down, Samantha." Duncan sounded colder than she'd ever heard him. "I want you here."

Sam lowered her voice as she turned to Duncan. "But I don't want to be here."

"Sit down," he repeated. "You're my wife. Whatever she has to say, she can say in front of you."

"You're making this much more difficult than it has to be, Duncan," said Lana, her huge brown eyes brimming with tears. "What I have to say might be a trifle upsetting to your new wife."

"What time is it?" Duncan asked Stephenson.

Stephenson checked his Rolex. "Half past six."

"You have three minutes Lana," Duncan said. "Start talking."

Lana looked so upset that Sam almost felt sorry for her. The woman turned to Stephenson, a pleading expression in her eyes, but the gentleman apparently had no help to offer. It was clear to Sam that Lana wanted her to leave but she didn't dare risk Duncan's wrath by trying a second time.

Never underestimate the recuperative powers of an actress. Lana closed her eyes for a second and when she opened them again, Sam would have sworn another woman had taken her place. This woman was poised, secure and self-confident. Not even the shadow of a pleading expression lingered in her eyes.

"Bryce and I went to get our marriage license yesterday," she said in a lilting, matter-of-fact voice.

Duncan shot the red-haired man a look of pity that embarrassed Sam. It had been years since he and Lana had divorced. They hadn't been married all that long when she left, and they'd never had children. The ties between them had been of the minor kind, easily cut with a simple divorce.

"That's hardly a new experience for you, Lana," he said, referring to her other failed attempts at matrimony.

"Actually, Duncan, it was a *very* new experience for me. This time they refused to grant me one."

Duncan looked briefly amused. "Maybe they're trying to tell you something."

"They did tell me something, Duncan," Lana said, her eyes flashing. "They said I'm still married to you."

Chapter Fourteen

Duncan leaped to his feet. "That's a lie."

"Exactly what I said," Lana responded, "but they had proof."

Sam watched, shell-shocked, as the dark-haired woman removed an envelope from her purse and handed it to Duncan.

"Go ahead," Lana said. "Read it. Then we'll talk."

Sam rose from her chair and moved toward Duncan as he opened the envelope, but he barely seemed to register her presence. "Duncan," she said. "What does it say?"

He didn't answer. He folded the letter and tossed it in Lana's direction. "You've been married two times since our divorce," he said, "and this is the first you've heard of this?"

Lana's smile was faintly condescending. "I *thought* I was married twice since our divorce. Apparently I was wrong."

"This is unacceptable," Duncan said.

"I couldn't agree more," said Lana.

"I can't say I'm pleased with the situation," Bryce Stephenson piped up.

Sam stepped forward. "And I—" That was the last thing she remembered.

SAM OPENED her eyes to find Duncan's ex-wife—no, make that his *current* wife—peering at her.

"I fainted?" Sam asked, struggling to sit up.

Lana nodded. "You're pregnant, aren't you?"

Sam placed a hand against her belly. "Yes, I am."

"How far along?"

Sam opted for vague truthfulness. "Not too terribly far."

"That explains a good deal," Lana said as Sam brushed her hair from her face. "Our Duncan did seem overly solicitous."

Sam bristled at the implication that only pregnancy could bring forth his solicitude. "Duncan is a kind man. He'd be concerned whether or not I was pregnant."

"You're loyal," Lana observed. "That's exactly what he likes. You two should get on well together."

Sam swung her feet to the floor. "Where is he?"

"Off to fetch you some water, I would think. Or the best medical care in Scotland." Lana's smile was amused. "I must say that was quite a display of husbandly concern he put on for us. He had you in his arms before you hit the floor, then set you down on the sofa like you were made of porcelain. That's the way he treated me when I was pregnant with his child."

Bile rose to Sam's throat, and for a moment she

feared she would be sick right there in the library. "You and Duncan have a child?"

Lana shook her head. "Things didn't work out," she said, her tone flat. "When the pregnancy ended, so did our marriage."

"There must have been more to it than that." That simply didn't sound like the man she'd come to know.

"Our Duncan is a simple man," Lana said, bitterness edging her words. "The baby meant everything to him, and once the baby was no more—" She snapped her fingers. "We were finished."

Sam stood up. If Lana was looking to undermine her self-confidence, she'd succeeded. "If you'll excuse me, I'm going upstairs to lie down for a while."

"I'm not trying to upset you, dear," Lana said. "I'm just telling you the truth, one Stewart wife to another."

"I'm not a Stewart wife," Sam said as the truth finally sank in. "I'm not a wife at all."

She stepped into the hallway. There was no sign of Duncan anywhere. She was halfway between the library and the staircase when she heard him and ducked behind the stairwell. Then Duncan's footsteps faded.

"Lassie, we need the Other One to move her car."

Sam jumped as Old Mag appeared at her side.

"What?" she asked, placing a hand over her rapidly pounding heart.

"The Other One's car is blocking the caterer. Would you ask her to do it? I wouldn't lower myself to talk with the likes of her."

"I don't want to talk to her either, Mag," Sam said

honestly. "Why don't I move it myself? If I remember right, they left the keys in the car."

"Aye," said Mag. "That would do." She looked closely at Sam. "Trouble, lassie?"

Sam nodded. "Trouble."

"Ach." Old Mag looked furious enough to commit murder. "Never thought I'd see the day she set foot in this house again."

The housekeeper's words seemed unbearably harsh to Sam. What had Lana done but lose a child? Was that all it took in this place to fall from grace? The thought sent a terrible chill up Sam's spine.

With one sentence, Lana had turned Sam's life inside out. Or had she just exposed Sam's life for what it really was? There had been no declarations of love between Sam and Duncan, only that miserable legal document that spelled out the details of their marriage.

So you'll marry him again, Sam. As soon as his divorce is legal.

They could ask the local priest or deacon to perform the ceremony. Maybe even invite a few guests. But why bother? It was only a business arrangement, after all. It had nothing whatever to do with love and never would. They could marry each other ten times over, and the result would always be the same—a marriage of convenience and nothing more.

He didn't love her. If he loved her, he would have told her so the day they heard their baby's heartbeat for the first time. If he loved her, he would have told her so last night, when she lay naked and sleepy in his arms. If he loved her, he could have told her so in the library when Lana broke the news.

But he didn't tell her he loved her, and for good reason.

Lana was right. Their marriage was about the baby and nothing else, and that was all it ever would be.

And, dear God, that wasn't enough.

She couldn't pretend any longer that it was. She wanted the whole package. She wanted passion. She wanted tenderness. She wanted someone whose eyes lit up with delight each time she walked into the room.

And she wanted it all with Duncan.

"I'll be out in a second to move the car, Mag," she said, then waited until the old woman went to the kitchen. She grabbed her purse from the desk drawer, made sure she had her passport and credit cards, then headed outside to the car.

Most of the partygoers had gone home, their enthusiasm dampened by Lana's unexpected arrival. A few people were gathered around the table where the whiskey bottles rested, but they didn't notice Sam as she slipped by and hurried toward Lana's car.

"I'll be paying my sitter overtime," the caterer called out through the open window of her truck. "I've been waiting forever to get out of here."

"Sorry," Sam said, forcing a smile. "Please add it to the bill."

She opened the door then slid behind the wheel of Lana's rental car. The keys were there, and the engine started up on the first try. A folded map lay on the dash with the road to Glasgow clearly highlighted in yellow. Omens didn't come any clearer than that.

Don't think, she told herself. *Just get as far away from here as you possibly can.*

She was an unmarried woman, after all.

She could go anywhere she wanted.

DUNCAN PUSHED OPEN the door to the library. "Where's Samantha?" he asked Lana as he glanced around the room.

Lana was curled in the corner of the leather couch, her small feet tucked under her. "Your almost-bride said she was going upstairs to lie down."

"How did she seem?"

Lana shrugged. "Fine. As well as any pregnant woman who just found out she wasn't married."

"How in bloody hell did you find out she was pregnant?"

"Duncan, darling, I have eyes. She's ripe as a peach, in case you haven't noticed."

Noticed? He'd memorized her curves with his fingertips, the palms of his hands, his tongue.

"Is this some trick of yours, Lana?" he asked. "Is there something you want besides the divorce?"

"Not a thing," she shot back so quickly that it left no doubt in his mind about her sincerity. "I want a divorce so I can marry Bryce."

"I'll call my lawyer after I check on Samantha."

"Your Samantha is fine, Duncan. She walked out of here under her own power. If you want to do something for her, let's get this thing resolved now."

He hesitated. What he wanted was to get Lana and her latest victim out of his house as fast as possible. He'd seen Samantha faint often enough to know how quickly she recovered. The fact that she'd felt well enough to leave the room proved that. Reluctantly he decided to stay.

"I'm calling my lawyer right now," he said to Lana, reaching for the telephone on the desk. "I suggest you do the same."

He'd be on his way to a second divorce before the sun rose again or know the reason why.

TWO HOURS LATER he had a set of instructions from his lawyer on how to proceed and the man's assurance that the problem could be easily solved.

Lana, dialing from one of her three cell phones, had a similar set from her lawyer.

"At least the two of you are in agreement about the divorce," Duncan's lawyer had said to him. "Quick and uncomplicated."

"With the emphasis on the former," Duncan had almost growled into the phone.

"As far as I can tell, darling, we can get this straightened out within a month," Lana said, obviously enjoying his annoyance.

"I'm going upstairs to tell Samantha."

He almost collided with Robby in the hallway.

"She's gone," Robby said. "I didn't want to tell you but Mag worries so."

Duncan stopped on the first step and looked at the older man. "Who's gone?"

"Your missus," Robby said, his narrow face pinched with worry. "She went to move the Other One's car two hours ago and we have not seen her since."

"What do you mean, you haven't seen her since?"

"The Other One blocked the caterer's car and Mag asked your missus if she'd be so kind to move it out of the way. Your missus is a sweet one and she said she would. The last we saw she was driving off down the road, happy as you please."

"Have you checked the bedroom?"

Robby's cheeks flamed bright red. "And what kind of man would you think I am?"

Duncan took the stairs two at a time. He threw open the bedroom door, praying he'd find Samantha asleep in bed, but the room was empty and silent. He went downstairs again and opened the top drawer of the desk where she kept her purse. His blood ran cold when he saw that it was missing. A woman didn't need her driver's license and credit cards to back a car down the driveway. But she would need those things if she had something more permanent in mind.

"I want you to call the police, Robby," he said as he strode toward the library. "Tell them Samantha is missing."

Lana, who was standing in the doorway to the library, glared at him over a tumbler of whiskey. "Missing?" she asked. "Don't you mean gone?"

"I don't have time for your nonsense," he said. "I have calls to make." He'd phone everyone in town, if necessary, on the chance that one of them might have seen Samantha.

"Just a minute here," Lana said. "Did I hear what the old man said correctly? She stole my car. I hope you won't forget to tell the police that small fact when you call them."

"Your car will show up when it shows up. It's my wife I'm worried about."

"Dare I remind you that she's not your wife and won't be until we settle this business between us.

Right now that car is a great deal more important to me than your runaway woman.''

''Samantha is missing,'' he said through tightly clenched teeth. ''I'd throw ten of your cars into Loch Glenraven if it meant getting her back.'' And if Lana was in one of them, so much the better. She didn't give a damn that Sam had gone missing. All she cared about was her rental car. Her friend Bryce, however, remained singularly unmoved by anything that was happening around them and sat, napping, in the wing chair.

''Good choice,'' Duncan said, tilting his head in Bryce's direction. ''You should be able to handle that one.''

''Bryce and I are marrying because we love each other,'' Lana said. She managed to sound righteously indignant. ''Not because he got me pregnant.''

''Take care, woman,'' he said, barely restraining his anger. ''What I share with Samantha is none of your concern.''

''You got what you wanted this time, didn't you, Duncan? A broodmare to give you a child.''

''By all that's holy, if you continue with this talk I won't be held accountable for my actions.''

''I told her about you, you know,'' Lana said. ''This obsession of yours with children seems to have worsened over the years. I must say, Samantha seemed to find it enlightening.''

''Did you tell her the whole story?'' Rage filled his throat like hot, acrid smoke. ''The way it really happened?''

''I told her the part she needed to know.''

He saw Lana down through the prism of years and wondered how it was he'd ever loved her. Her beauty was born of selfishness and anger. Samantha's beauty was born of kindness and hope. When he was a younger man he might not have understood the distinction. Now that he was approaching the midpoint of life, it meant everything.

He reached for the telephone and was about to punch in a number when he was struck by a thought.

"Where did you go when we broke up?" he asked Lana without preamble.

She frowned slightly. "To Rome, I think. Filming was about to start and—"

"Before Rome," he interrupted. "I'm talking about the day our marriage ended." That night of despair and broken dreams.

"I went home to my mother."

He stepped out into the hallway and bellowed for Old Mag.

"You're loud enough to wake the dead, laddie," she scolded him. "What is it you want?"

"Think back, old woman," he said. "To the beginning. When you and Robby had a dust-up, where did you go?"

Mag drew herself up to her full height. "I never once left my husband's house," she said proudly. "But Robby went home to his mam more than once."

Sam and her mother weren't close, but they had been in contact lately. Besides, Julia was her only relative in Great Britain. Where else would she go?

And, more important, how quickly could he get there?

London, later that same night

"SAMANTHA!" Julia peered through the partially open door of her Kensington flat. "What on earth?"

"Are you going to let me in, Mother, or shall I spend what's left of the night on your doorstep?"

Julia, clutching her pale rose silk kimono to her breast, didn't move an inch. "Is your husband with you?"

"Haven't you heard?" Sam asked. "I don't have a husband. Now will you please let me in?"

"No husband!" The door swung wide open. "Darling, that's the best thing I've heard in weeks."

"You're a wonder, Mother," Sam muttered as she stepped into the hallway. She tossed her purse on the small mahogany table positioned beneath a rococo mirror. Even in the middle of the night with her face still bruised from cosmetic surgery, Julia managed to look better than most women did on their best days. "I thought you said you looked too terrible to come to our party."

"I do," Julia said, locking the door behind Sam. "Now what was that you said about no husband?"

"You heard me." Sam stalked in the general direction of the living room. "Your prayers were answered. I am no longer a married woman."

Julia claimed one end of the flowery chintz sofa and gestured for Sam to claim the other end. "That doesn't happen in one day, darling. What's the story?"

Sam sat down for a split second then jumped up again. Her adrenaline was flowing too fast for her to stay still. "It's actually quite a simple story, Mother. You can't have two wives at one time."

"Two wives?"

"You remember Lana, don't you? After all, you were the one who told me all about how much my husband loved her."

"Oh, my God," Julia exclaimed. "They're back together?"

Sam made a face of disgust. "Only in the legal sense. You see, Mother, Lana wants to marry a man named Bryce and she can't do that if she's still married to one named Duncan."

"What a wonderful mess," Julia said, looking positively delighted. "I was praying you'd come to your senses and now you don't have to. Your marriage is over."

With that Sam burst into loud tears.

"Darling!" Julia was beside her in an instant. "Whatever are you crying about? That was a marriage of convenience, not a love match. You don't need a man to help you bring up your baby. You have me and you have your father and your sisters. We'll help you."

Sam sank onto the edge of the sofa and cried all the harder.

"Now, now," said Julia awkwardly. Her maternal skills were practically nonexistent. For Julia, this was the equivalent of twenty years of mothering crammed into one ten-minute period. "He wasn't right for you anyway, darling. I'm sure he and that terrible Lana creature are right now—"

"Mother!" The word tore from Sam's throat in desperation. "Haven't you understood one single word I've said? I love Duncan Stewart."

Julia sighed. "I wish you wouldn't say things like that."

"I love Duncan," Sam repeated, amazed at how easy it was to say the words.

"And when did you come to this amazing conclusion?"

"I don't know," she said honestly. "All I know is that I do."

"I hope to heaven he doesn't know anything about this."

"I should have told him," Sam murmured, more to herself than to her mother.

"Never tell a man something like that," Julia cried out. "My God, Samantha, don't you know anything about being a woman? You can't give a man the advantage that way."

"You never told Daddy that you loved him?"

"My one mistake," Julia said, "and see how it ended. Divorced before I knew it."

"Mother," said Sam, "you also had a boyfriend. I think that might have contributed to the situation."

"A symptom, not a cause," Julia said, unmoved by Sam's logic. "I'm older than you, darling. I understand the way it is between men and women better than you ever could. The best thing you did was to keep your emotions to yourself. Now, at least, you don't have to worry about being embarrassed."

"I wouldn't be embarrassed."

Julia looked at her in horror. "Well, now I understand why you've been single so long."

"No, you don't, Mother," Sam said. "You haven't the foggiest idea."

Julia was not a woman comfortable with confrontation. "Darling, you look exhausted," she said, rising to her feet. "Why don't I make you some warm milk then tuck you in for a nice long nap? You must think about the baby.''

Tears sprang to Sam's eyes. "You don't have to do that, Mother," she said.

"Indulge me," Julia said. "I know I haven't been a very good mother to you, Samantha. At least let me try to learn how to be a good grandmother."

Sam nodded, too emotional to speak. What a strange twenty-four hours it had been. She watched as her mother left the room, wondering what bizarre twist of fate had decided to bestow maternal instincts on Julia at this late date. Or make Sam feel like her daughter.

She leaned her head back against the sofa and closed her eyes. She saw Glenraven rising up from the Scottish mist. She saw Old Mag and Robby. She saw their wonderful friends and neighbors toasting their happiness.

But no matter how hard she tried, she couldn't quite see Duncan.

She supposed she should be grateful to Lana for forcing her to take a clear-eyed look at the situation. She loved Duncan and he didn't love her.

And nothing on heaven or earth would ever change that.

JULIA'S FLAT was less than two blocks from Kensington Palace, one of London's better areas. Duncan, however, was not in the mood to be impressed by its royal ambience. The only thing he cared about was finding Samantha.

The doorman to Julia's building blocked his entrance. "May I ask who you're here to see, sir?"

"Julia," Duncan said. Bloody hell. He couldn't remember her last name. He manufactured a man-to-man smile. "The one and only Julia."

The doorman smiled at him. "And you are?"

"Expected," Duncan said.

"I'll need a name."

"Tell her Duncan Stewart is here."

The doorman nodded then went off to use the house phone.

Minutes later Duncan stood in front of Julia's door. The gold and silver wedding ring was in his pocket. His heart, however, was on his sleeve.

Samantha's mother took her sweet time opening up for him. For a moment Duncan wondered if he'd missed his guess and his bride had gone home to Texas after all, but the moment he saw Julia's face he knew he'd come to the right place.

"I want to see Samantha," he said, bypassing a polite introduction.

"She doesn't want to see you."

"Let her tell me that and then I'll go."

"You have no rights over my daughter," Julia said, glaring at him.

"I don't want any rights over your daughter," he said. "I want to talk to her."

"She's asleep."

"Then I'd ask you to wake her up."

"And I'm asking you to leave." Julia's eyes narrowed. "You're not her husband any longer, Mr. Stewart."

He felt as if he'd been dealt a body blow. "I love her," he said, dropping his pride at her feet.

"Oh, Mr. Stewart," Julia said, with a sigh. "How I wish you hadn't said that...."

SAM WAS THUMBING through a copy of *Tatler* when she heard the knock on her door. So far Julia had been an unending source of warm milk, buttered toast and good intentions. Being mothered was a new experience for Sam, and although she had had her fill of all three commodities, she didn't want to discourage Julia.

"Come in, Mother," she called, not looking up from her magazine. She heard the door squeak open, then heavy footsteps.

"I've come to take you home, Samantha."

Duncan.

The world seemed to suddenly narrow into nothing more than the sound of his voice. Hands trembling, she turned the page.

"Go away," she said. "I am home."

She could feel his presence in every part of her body. He charged the atmosphere in the room simply by being there.

"Look at me, lassie."

"Why should I?" she countered, longing to do exactly that. "It's not like you're my husband or anything."

He sat next to her on the bed. She turned away from him.

"I love you, Samantha."

His words grabbed her by the heart and wouldn't let go. "Don't," she whispered. *Don't play games like that, Duncan.* Did he have any idea how easy it would be to break her heart with words he didn't mean? "You really should go."

"Not until you look at me, lassie." He brushed the hair from her cheek with a gentle hand. "Not until you listen to what I have to say."

She turned to face him, and the expression in his beautiful eyes was almost her undoing. Hope, foolish hope, sprang to life inside her heart and no matter how hard she tried to control it, that hope continued to grow.

"I'm listening," she said.

"I love you, lassie. I believe I've loved you from that first moment in the plane when you stormed out on me, determined to find your own way to Glen-raven."

He reached for her hand, the one with the signet ring she hadn't been able to bring herself to take off. His fingers locked with hers and she didn't pull away. Wisps of hope. Pieces of dreams. And one very important question.

"That's infatuation," she said at last. "That isn't love."

"It's how love begins. When the plane hit trouble, I saw who you really were. A brave woman with more heart and courage than twenty men."

A small smile tilted her mouth. "And you fell in love with my bravery?"

"Aye, that and more. With your beauty and your bravery. With your heart and with your soul."

"You knew nothing of me, Duncan. How could you possibly love what you didn't know?"

He told her of an evening in a little pub outside Glasgow. About a man who spotted his loneliness and called him on it. A man who made him see the empty shell his life would be without her by his side.

"You never wondered why I followed you to Texas? You never thought about that?"

"At first I thought you wanted your ten thousand dollars," she said.

"And then?"

She shrugged. "And then it was about the baby."

"I had no way of knowing about the baby, Samantha. I came to Texas for you."

How could she have forgotten that? The night of her sister's wedding was such a blur of emotion that somehow she'd managed to overlook the fact that he'd traveled from the Highlands all the way to Houston to see her again. To hear her voice. The baby's existence had been unknown to both of them.

He had come to see Sam.

She struggled to rein in her feelings.

"Lana—" She stopped, unable to continue over the swell of emotion inside her heart.

"What did Lana tell you?"

"She told me about the baby—" She swallowed. "Your baby, the one you lost."

His expression turned dark, and she drew back instinctively. "That's what she told you, is it? That we *lost* the baby?"

"Yes," Sam said, bewildered. "A miscarriage. And that once she'd lost the baby, you had no more use for her." That all he'd wanted from the marriage was a child of his own.

"It wasn't a miscarriage, Samantha." He met her eyes. "She aborted our baby without my knowledge."

His pain seemed to flood her body and she closed her eyes against it. She'd never known a man's voice could hold such terrible grief. "My God, Duncan...I had no idea."

"Neither had I," he said. "She was two months pregnant and she said she was as happy about it as I was. A movie role came along and she went down to London to audition. When she came to Glenraven a week later, she had the job but she didn't have the baby. A 'business decision,' she called it."

It explained so much about him. The steadiness of his support, right from the start. His devotion to their unborn child. But did it explain his love for her?

"I'm so sorry," she whispered. To lose both wife and child through a selfish, impulsive decision, taken with no consideration whatsoever for his feelings on the matter.

The experience had changed him, he told her. He withdrew into his studio. He lost faith in love. His interludes with women were based on physical attraction, not the possibility of love. His heart had closed itself off to the world.

"And then I met you, lassie, and the sun came out again."

She wanted to believe him. With her entire heart and soul, she longed to throw herself into his arms and give herself up to the hope and wonder of love. But she had to be sure, both for her sake and the sake of their baby.

"I thought we were doing the right thing when we got married, Duncan," she began, choosing her words with great care. "I believed that a marriage of convenience was possible, that two intelligent people could put aside their personal concerns for the greater good.'' She drew in a steadying breath. ''For the good of our baby.''

His eyes were shadowed, his expression impossible to read. ''And what is it you think now, Samantha?''

She couldn't stop the flow of tears that rolled down her cheeks. ''I think we made a mistake. Marriage should be between two people who love each other, Duncan. It's not a business arrangement. It can't be reduced to a stack of legal documents.''

Duncan turned away from her. Had she reached into his heart and tore it from his chest, she could not have hurt him more.

''Duncan.'' Her voice pierced the web of regret that had settled itself over him. ''You're not listening to me.''

''I heard every word, lassie,'' he said. Each of those words had left their mark on his soul.

''I want us to start over,'' she said. ''Did you hear me say that?''

He met her eyes one more time. ''To what purpose?''

''To what purpose?'' She spread her arms wide. ''Don't you know?''

''I want you to tell me.'' He wanted her to say the words he'd longed to hear her say from the first moment they met.

Her cornflower blue eyes grew soft and dreamy, the way they had after he made love to her. It was almost his undoing.

''I love you, Duncan.'' Her tentative smile widened and lit up her lovely face with radiant light. ''I don't know when it started. I don't know why it took me so long to realize it. But I love you." She gripped his hand more tightly. "With my entire heart and soul."

She told him she wanted a real marriage, the kind that was based on love and mutual respect. She wanted them to be a family in every sense of the word, to raise their children in love and hope and joy.

She wanted them to try again.

She moved into his arms and his mouth found hers. Their kiss was sweet, reverential, as filled with wonder as the sound of a child's laughter.

For Sam, it was like walking from the darkness into the light. From cold winter into the shimmering warmth of summer.

From an uncertain present to a miraculous future she'd never believed possible.

He broke the kiss and she murmured her protest against his lips. The smell of his skin, the sweet taste of his mouth were intoxicating. She loved everything about him, heart and soul and body.

"Duncan?" He stood and reached deep into the pocket of his trousers. "What are you doing?"

"This," he said, then dropped to his knee next to the bed. "Marry me, Samantha." He flipped open the lid of the box and withdrew a breathtaking ring of intertwined gold and silver. "Marry me because I love you and you love me in equal measure. Marry me because when we're not together life loses its luster and its meaning."

She held out her hand and he placed the ring in her palm.

"There's an inscription," he said. The emotion in his voice was unmistakable, and her heart soared.

She held the ring under the lamplight and saw her new initials and his and the date of their wedding.

"When did you do this?" she asked. Certainly there hadn't been time tonight.

"I picked it up the day before the party," he said. "I'd planned to give it to you after all the guests left." He paused. "After I finally told you that I loved you."

The last of her doubts vanished in one wild burst of joy. She moved the signet ring to her right hand then handed the silver-and-gold band to him. "I want you to put it on my finger," she said. "To make this official."

He slid the ring onto her finger with all the ceremony it deserved then made her gasp when he kissed the palm of her hand then folded each finger over the spot. Her Highland warrior. Her Scots poet.

Her husband.

If someone had told her this time last year that she would give her heart to a stranger on a windswept day in Scotland, she would have thought him mad. But she had, and that one moment of passion had changed her life forever. She'd discovered she knew how to love passionately and well and that, even with its difficulties, a real marriage between equals was the grandest adventure on earth. They were both opinionated and stubborn, as much prone to argument as discussion. Their marriage would be a fiery one but it would never be dull. Not as long as they loved each other. And somehow she knew they would love each other until the end of time.

She opened her mouth to say exactly that, then stopped.

"Samantha?" He leaned forward, his look of joy sliding into one of concern. "Is something wrong, lassie?"

She shook her head, motioning for him to be still.

"Oh, Duncan!" She reached for his hands then placed them on the roundness of her belly.

His brows knit together in a frown then suddenly he leaped back, as if burned. "Is that—"

"Yes!" she exclaimed, laughing and crying at the same time. "The baby, Duncan. Our baby moved!"

That flutter against his palms, that almost imperceptible ripple—that was their baby, his and Samantha's, waiting to be born. If he'd ever doubted the existence of angels, Duncan doubted it no more.

Angels were everywhere. He knew that now. Sometimes they came in the guise of a lovely blond American in need of a ride to Glenraven. Sometimes they came in the form of a baby, curled deep within its mother's womb.

And sometimes, if a man was very lucky, he was smart enough to hold tight when he found his angels, and never let them go.

Duncan drew Samantha and their baby into his arms and held on tight.

EVER HAD ONE OF THOSE DAYS?

TO DO:

☑ at the supermarket buying two dozen muffins that your son just remembered to tell you he needed for the school treat, you realize you left your wallet at home

☑ at work just as you're going into the big meeting, you discover your son took your presentation to school, and you have his hand-drawn superhero comic book

☑ your mother-in-law calls to say she's coming for a month-long visit

☑ finally at the end of a long and exasperating day, you escape from it all with an entertaining, humorous and always romantic Love & Laughter book!

ENJOY
LOVE & LAUGHTER™
EVERY DAY!

For a preview, turn the page....

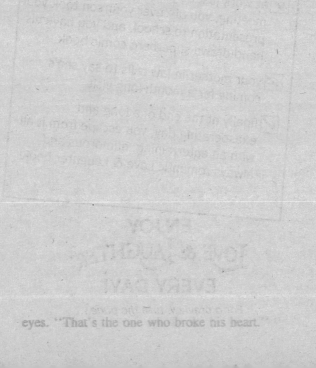

eyes. "That's the one who broke his heart."

*Here's a sneak peek at
Carrie Alexander's THE AMOROUS HEIRESS
Available September 1997...*

"YOU'RE A VERY popular lady," Jed Kelley observed as Augustina closed the door on her suitors.

She waved a hand. "Just two of a dozen." Technically true since her grandmother had put her on the open market. "You're not afraid of a little competition, are you?"

"Competition?" He looked puzzled. "I thought the position was mine."

Augustina shook her head, smiling coyly. "You didn't think Grandmother was the final arbiter of the decision, did you? I say a trial period is in order." No matter that Jed Kelley had miraculously passed Grandmother's muster, Augustina felt the need for a little propriety. But, on the other hand, she could be married before the summer was out and be free as a bird, with the added bonus of a husband it wouldn't be all that difficult to learn to love.

She got up the courage to reach for his hand, and then just like that, she—Miss Gussy Gutless Fairchild—was holding Jed Kelley's hand. He looked down at their linked hands. "Of course, you don't really know what sort of work I can do, do you?"

A funny way to put it, she thought absently, cradling his callused hand between both of her own. "We can get to know each other, and then, if that works out..." she murmured. *Wow*. If she'd known what this arranged marriage thing was all about, she'd have been a supporter of Grandmother's campaign from the start!

"Are you a palm reader?" Jed asked gruffly. His voice was as raspy as sandpaper and it was rubbing her all the right ways, but the question flustered her. She dropped his hand.

"I'm sorry."

"No problem," he said, "as long as I'm hired."

"Hired!" she scoffed. "What a way of putting it!"

Jed folded his arms across his chest. "So we're back to the trial period."

"Yes." Augustina frowned and her gaze dropped to his work boots. Okay, so he wasn't as well off as the majority of her suitors, but really, did he think she was going to *pay* him to marry her?

"Fine, then." He flipped her a wave and, speechless, she watched him leave. She was trembling all over like a malaria victim in a snowstorm, shot with hot charges and cold shivers until her brain was numb. This couldn't be true. Fantasy men didn't happen to nice girls like her.

"Augustina?"

Her grandmother's voice intruded on Gussy's privacy. "Ahh. There you are. I see you met the new gardener?"